GINGERBREAD PEOPLE

Gingerbread People

Alexey Williams

ISBN 979-8-9873743-2-0
Available as an electronic book; ISBN 979-8-9873743-3-7

First Printing, 2023

Cover image: *The Knock-Out*, Luc-Albert Moreau, 1927; National Gallery of Ireland

In a large bowl, whisk together flour,
ginger, cloves, nutmeg, baking soda,
baking powder, and salt; set aside.

Martha Stewart

CONTENTS

1

APRIL 7, 2009

We went into the hotel and I was surprised to see the photographs of the bloodied boxers framed and hanging from the wall, but then I remembered Yvan knew the hotel owner from his boxing days. She'd been the girlfriend of a promoter when Yvan was fighting back East, and Yvan told me later that she still held matches in the hotel's semi-basement when she had young men she wanted to pair. Bare knuckle. A man named Pierre Marie manned the hotel's front desk when Sherry was not around, and I've always remembered his name because I thought there was something very French and Catholic about having a first name from a male saint and a second from the Virgin. I met Pierre Marie shortly after Yvan and I arrived at the hotel. We were talking to Sherry and this tall man in tight jeans marched down from the second floor of the hotel holding a tray of sliced meats and bread. Pierre Marie set the tray down at the counter, pushing aside the rifle that Sherry kept there, and I saw his skinless knuckles and cauliflower ears. Yvan told me that men don't get cauliflower ears from boxing so Pierre Marie must have been a grappler. Men get ears like that when other men break the cartilage and blood vessels in the ear while grappling and the ears don't heal properly.

Sherry told Pierre Marie that Yvan and I were on the run, and Yvan said: "Charlotte's not on the run. She's with me. For all the police know, I kidnapped her. I forced her to get married and then I kidnapped her." Yvan explained that he'd managed to sell the reliquary he had stolen, but it hadn't been enough to buy a different car and all the other things we needed so he'd robbed a bank. We'd come to the hotel to hide out, and there was a feeling of pity in the room after Yvan told the meatier parts of our story to Sherry and Pierre Marie. The pity was mostly for me.

"I was thinking of you today after Yvan called," Sherry said to me, and she handed me a blue teddy bear little larger than the palm of my hand from behind the counter.

The wall behind the hotel check-in counter was ringed with teddy bears of various sizes. Sherry said Pierre Marie had won them at the county fair. They kept them around to gift to customers they particularly liked. Customers could also buy them if they wanted. Sherry and Pierre Marie were both tall and good looking, but I didn't think they were together. Sherry had a down-by-the-docks manner of speaking, but she was beautiful and her looks drew your attention because of a kind of bloody glow her skin had, like someone's flushed face after they'd been in a fight. I immediately felt that I could trust her, and after the police lost track of us, which we knew from the sound of the sirens dying down, she took me by the hand and led me to where she lived, which was a mobile home parked behind the hotel. As Sherry began to lead me away, Yvan mentioned that he had to go back out to the wilds since he needed to use some of the cash we had from the bank to buy a used car. It had always been his intention to swap cars when we reached here. Yvan called the town outside the hotel the wilds. Before Yvan left, he walked over to me and whispered that he'd left a gun in the kitchen if I needed it. Sherry told Pierre Marie not to go with Yvan but to plant himself in the entryway in case someone came to check-in to the hotel, although she admitted it was the slow season. If anyone who looked like a plain-clothes police officer came around, Pierre Marie was to hang a "No Vacancies" sign in the window.

"It's better if you stay up front, Marie," said Yvan. "Don't follow me out."

To Yvan, Pierre Marie was always just Marie. Yvan left, and Sherry led me away. The metal steps up to her trailer creaked as we scaled them, and beside the short flight of stairs was a statue of a brown bear holding a honeycomb. A television played in Sherry's trailer, and on the screen a beautiful young woman walks inside a trailer in front of which stands a bear holding a honeycomb. There was something warm and engaging about Sherry and I found her easy to talk to. She told me she'd been a semi-professional ice skater when she was younger, so we had that in common. Sherry said she'd also dated criminals when she was younger, and that made me wince as I didn't see Yvan that way. He was still the boxer that wanted to be a priest as far as I was concerned. Anything else that people might say was just slander. Until recently the kind of milieu that Sherry referred to was as foreign to Yvan as it was to me, even if Yvan had spent several years as an amateur boxer in college. A world where people stole horses and put sugar in gas tanks. Then Sherry told me about all the infamous people she'd encountered when she was younger, and she rummaged through a drawer where she removed a picture of a famous boxer that'd been stuck between the pages of a magazine. Some magazines have perfume samples and things can get stuck to the glue they use to fold the page. Sherry took out the magazine too, tossing the heavy thing onto a stool. She explained that her mobile home had four large rooms, and then she asked me how I'd met Yvan since he hadn't said anything to her about it when she'd spoken to him on the phone.

2

AUGUST 7, 2008

I told Sherry the events surrounding how I'd moved to Yvan's town, and that meant I had to tell her about Paul Boyer, since I'd met him first. I'd only met Yvan later. It seemed silly to start with Paul since his appearance in my life had been so brief, but I'd only crossed paths with Yvan because of Paul. Paul had been the first person I'd met when I arrived in town, as I'd met him even before the landlady. My father hadn't wanted me to move here, and after he'd driven me to the bus station, he said: "You know what happened to Dawn after she moved out of her parents' house. She ended up at Alexian Brothers Hospital. She got engaged to a guy she met at a bar, and he abandoned her at a bus station the first chance he got. By then she was pregnant. She gave birth to a dead baby, and next thing anyone knew she was being committed to the psychiatric floor at Alexian Brothers. I don't want that happening to you, Charlotte." I told him that he'd never have to commit me to Alexian Brothers Hospital like Dawn, and I reminded him that my stepmother had made dinner and was waiting for him at home. Standing by the driver's side window, I kissed him on the cheek and he drove off. After the bus dropped me in town, I called the landlady who explained she was running late. We'd arranged for her to pick me up from the bus station.

As I had the time, I left the station and wandered to the nearby site of the fairgrounds, which was closed for the week. The concession stands had their doors and windows shut. A path led past the minor attractions before you reached the Ferris wheel and the helter skelter. Most of these attractions were in wooden buildings that looked slapdash in the waning light of afternoon, and a gaggle of high school girls walking past in miniskirts seemed to agree. There weren't any strings of lights and lanterns to give the space the glare of activity it had at night, and I found myself walking hastily along the path to a clearing near the funhouse where a pair of tables sat. Before sitting at a table, I turned around and noted an old woman moving slowly towards me. She must have followed me the whole while, I just hadn't seen her. When she reached me, she said: "You don't belong here, sweetie. You're too sweet for this place." She was dressed too warmly for the weather, and she pushed a baby carriage filled with baby dolls with melted faces. I didn't know what to say to her, and by the time I'd come up with something she'd already gone.

After she left, I watched the garish face that'd been built on the side of the funhouse. The face had a mouth that swallowed the door and above this a hellish nose and eyes. Anyone who walked through the funhouse door would be walking right into the devil's mouth. I hadn't been looking at the face long when I noticed a blond-haired man fast approaching with his long legs. When he reached me, he asked me how I'd gotten into the fairgrounds. I told him I'd dipped under the chain and pushed open the doors to the fairgrounds just like anyone would have done, like he must have done. The doors hadn't been locked. He told me I was sitting in his spot, but he was smiling and laughing as he said it. This was Paul Boyer. He sat across from me and told me that I didn't have to worry about come-ons since he was preparing for the priesthood.

"And priests don't come on to people?" I asked.

"They're not supposed to," said Paul. "I'm at the seminary. Don't you know about the seminary? I guess not."

"I just moved here. I don't know anything."

"Ah, fresh meat," said Paul.

"Oh God, don't say that."

"Well, it's true. Someone like you is just asking for trouble."

I said: "What is that supposed to mean?" but then I laughed and told Paul that he was probably right. It wasn't revealing too much to tell Paul that my father hadn't wanted me to move here alone. He was convinced I'd meet the wrong man and give birth to a stillborn baby.

"Well, there's no way that's true," said Paul. "No one gives birth to stillborn babies anymore."

"No?"

"No. Stick with me and you'll be all right. You'll meet some of the guys from the seminary, and at least you'll know some people."

"So I guess all the students live at the seminary."

"Nah, most of them do," said Paul.

He asked me a few questions about myself, and I told him about my Master's in French. This interested him as the seminarians had to learn it. If Paul was to be believed, most of the guys could barely get by with English, let alone learn another language. He removed his wallet to show me a picture of some of his friends, and I laughed since I didn't see what that had to do with what he'd just told me. It didn't matter to me which men specifically were having trouble with French and whether they were his friends or not. He handed me the photo and I had a good look at it. One of the men in the photo was Yvan, but I hadn't met Yvan yet. Yvan was the best looking one. As I inspected the picture, Paul passed a few fingers through his closely-cropped hair.

"I'm sure my landlady's here by now," I told Paul, and I stood up from the table where we sat. "I'm meeting her at the bus station."

We introduced ourselves, and I explained that I'd found a job in town and was living with an older woman, at least until I found another place. She was giving me a ride as I didn't know the town well enough to walk. Paul took my phone number and suggested we meet up later in the week. He said: "There's this thing at St. Vincent's on Thursday that you might like. I'll call you." The wind rattled the few trees that had been planted in the space, dwarfed by the funhouse, the Ferris wheel and the helter skelter. We agreed to meet up later. Then I marched away from the angry, sinister face on the side of the funhouse and Paul reached into his bag to remove his theology textbook. He'd come to study after all. God was in the pages.

When I reached the room I was renting with the landlady, she said: "This room's the perfect size for you, Charlotte. And I don't mind gentlemen callers, but no overnight guests." I smiled at this old-fashioned way to refer to boys, and I nodded my understanding. I didn't tell her that the only person I knew was a priest, or at least a man studying to be one. The house seemed all right until I met the other inmates that lived there, for that's what we were. The landlady was our prison warden. Someone had scratched "Get laid, bitch" into her door, and she'd tried to rub it clean with bleach and Pledge, but you could still make out the words. She lived in a large apartment on the first floor and would often appear to harass me when I didn't think she was home. The job I'd told Paul about was at a diner, though I hoped to find clients looking for a French tutor. I'd registered as a substitute teacher at the school, but I didn't expect much to come from that. The landlady herself told me that it took months for the school to call in new substitutes, and by then I was sure I wouldn't care about it anymore. I'd already forgotten about the school when Paul called me the day before the party. This was the party at St. Vincent's that he'd told me about outside the funhouse. He arranged a time for us to meet. He'd pick me up at the house and we'd drive together. On the day in question, I spent an hour in front of the mirror even though it was just Paul.

"You look nice," Paul said politely in the car.

He playfully flicked the pine-scented air freshener with a finger and made it clear that it wasn't a date, which I already knew. Paul asked me about my family and I told him that my mother died years ago and my father had remarried a woman from Europe who owned a travel agency. She was very beautiful and always looked nice, but there was a persistent rumor that she'd worked in a brothel before she met my father. That's how she'd gotten the money to purchase the travel agency, from a wealthy man she'd met at the brothel. Paul chuckled and I knew it was because *brothel* was such an old-fashioned word. I didn't know what else to call it. She was a sex worker who used to work at a brothel. Her name was Laura and we weren't close. I avoided family gatherings where I knew I'd run into her, but I didn't tell Paul that. I only told him that I'd been close to my father, but things had changed since my mother had died. After Paul parked the car in the large lot at St. Vincent's, I tilted the rear-view mirror down to make sure my hair hadn't been flattened by the rain. It had begun to drizzle while I'd stood outside waiting for Paul's Suzuki to arrive.

"I didn't tell you that St. Vincent's was a former mental hospital," Paul said as we sat in the car, turning his face sheepishly toward mine.

"Oh, that's great. My father will love that."

"Ha. I'm sorry."

"No, it's fine," I laughed. "I already knew St. Vincent's used to be a psych hospital. I asked the landlady about it yesterday and she told me. She said it was a mental hospital that some lunatic turned into apartments. Not a former patient, but another lunatic. You know, just out of their mind. The landlady knows the property manager, and I regretted asking her about the place because she spent the next hour and a half complaining about this lady. The manager's name is Mrs. Havermeyer or something. Do you know her?"

"No."

"Anyway, I need to move soon because I don't think the landlady likes me," I told Paul.

"Impossible."

"Right? I'm always running into her in the hallway and she'll tell me I'm pretty, but she says it like it's a charge. Like she's the judge and I'm charged with being pretty."

"I'm sure that's not how she means it," said Paul. "I don't know, if you need another place to live, there's lots of apartment buildings downtown that are renting. In fact, you can probably get a better deal than what you're getting at that house where you're at now."

Paul mentioned that some of the seminarians from the photo he'd shown me would be at the party. Frank, Wayne, Yvan. The brickwork outside St. Vincent's had been repaired and the trees improved, but the place was still grim like an old hospital. As we walked up the steps, Paul's face was cast into prominence by the harsh white street lighting, and I couldn't help but see him as someone's boyfriend rather than a priest. There was something worldly about him, but not as worldly as Yvan would be. Sherry laughed at this observation as if she knew all about it. I wondered if she'd dated Yvan when he was younger, but I couldn't possibly ask her that. As I walked with Paul to the elevator, he told me that we'd have to take the stairs part of the way since the elevator didn't go up to five. The fifth floor was shut off from the rest of the building because something horrible had happened there.

The stairwell between the fourth and fifth floor was covered in graffiti, and I was surprised that it hadn't occurred to Mrs. Havermeyer to paint it over in a new coat of awful yellow paint. The innards of the building were covered in this awful yellow paint. There were already people gathered on the fifth floor when we reached it. They were couples mostly, but occasionally we came across men that walked the floor alone. I assumed these must be seminarians like Paul. Many of them were shy and wore glasses. Paul said: "The person throwing the party lives in this building. I think they invited me and some of the other guys because there's supposed to be this scary chapel up here. They don't know where it is, but I bet it's in one of the round towers." Paul told me that the mental unit of St. Vincent's had been run entirely by a religious order, which I didn't believe until we walked past a framed picture of a very displeased-looking nun.

"What's up, Sister Mary Alphonse," Paul said as we walked past her. He patted her face in the frame playfully.

"Is that her name?" I asked.

"I don't know," said Paul.

We walked toward a group of people that Paul knew and he introduced me. They all got to talking and I glanced around the floor. The fifth floor had retained the look of a hospital with its white walls and laminate flooring. The cramped-like-a-shoebox rooms remained as they'd been when the inpatients had slept in them, and this gave the space a left-for-dead quality. Paul grabbed a glass of wine for me and led me to a seat by the window. He didn't drink since he was tasked with driving us home later. It was suddenly cold and I shivered. Paul noticed that a window near us was cracked and he leapt up to close it. I was still ice cold and I remarked that Paul had dressed more appropriately for the weather than I had. I flattened a crease in my dress. It was really a button-up dress shirt like one that a man would wear only it came to my knees and was cinched in with a belted. Paul asked me if I liked town and I told I didn't know yet. I'd only met him really. Paul stood up when someone at the far end of the room shouted his name. He shouted it the way boys shout their friends' names at frat parties. Distant car horns honked on the road and a tree branch outside thrashed against the window.

I left the space soon afterward and walked the halls. It wasn't long before I found Yvan. He was alone and flexing and un-flexing his palms. The room he was sitting in was larger than the others. It had a mullioned window that looked out onto the parking lot and the walls were lined with empty shelves. I sat beside Yvan on a fake leather couch that faced the window.

I thought I had to say something, so I said: "Paul told me there's a chapel up here. That's why they invited everyone."

"That's not why they invited everyone," Yvan said, not looking at me. "Some really bad things happened up here. They wanted us to see where the depposession took place."

"The depossession?"

"The exorcism," said Yvan. "Here, look at this," and Yvan jumped up from the couch.

I followed him to the bookshelf. The bookshelf wasn't as free of books as I'd thought. Yvan found a book with a green spine and gold lettering that he removed from the shelf. The binding had been warped by water damage, but Yvan adeptly flipped through the pages. I was surprised by how calloused his hands were, but these only served to set Yvan apart from Paul. Yvan's callouses were thick and red: like sex organs rising out of his palms. In the book he showed me a picture of an imagined depossession ordered by the Church.

As I examined the picture, Yvan said: "So you came here with Paul?"

I told him that I had come with Paul, but it wasn't a date.

"Of course, it's not a date," said Yvan. "Paul's supposed to be a priest one day."

I glanced at Yvan, but he looked away. I was cold again and I used my hands to rub my arms and shoulders, which were partially exposed in my shirt dress.

"Here," said Yvan, and he took off his leather jacket and lowered it around my back and shoulders.

Yvan told me that he'd been an amateur boxer before he'd decided to become a priest. That explained his hands and his nose. His nose was slightly crooked like it'd been broken once and not properly realigned.

His knuckles were raw. I imagined his bedroom at the seminary. It was filled with remnants of his former life: boxing gloves, straps, red polyester shorts. The boxing gloves hung from a nail in the wall and told the story of a boy who didn't know who he was and was trying to find out. He had fast hands but not much else.

We didn't remain long at St. Vincent's. I looked for the chapel with Yvan, but we never found it. Yvan took up Paul's idea to search the towers, but all we found were the disturbed writings of the people that had lived there: written on the walls and on shredded bed sheets. Yvan said he wanted to show me a place nearby and we left where we were, taking the stairs all the way down to the entrance. Yvan said there was an abandoned house nearby and there were many houses like that in town because there weren't as many people here as there'd been once. It was a mill town and no one really milled anymore. There'd once been mills everywhere, but now there was just the one: located a mile or two outside of town. As Yvan walked with me to this abandoned house, he shadow boxed with himself on the street. His adroitness didn't surprise me because there was something very physical about him. A man driving a horse and buggy passed us as we walked, and I saw the shadow of the man and his horse trotting along with the silhouettes of Yvan and me. Later they broke into a gallop. Yvan told me that there was an Amish community outside of town and sometimes the men drove in late at night to deliver the goods from their farms.

When we reached the house, Yvan tried to shove in the door to open it. Rain and mold had warped the door, and when it wouldn't budge Yvan kicked it. The house was filled with small horse figurines and paintings of horses. There was a child's rocking horse as you approached the kitchen. The people that had lived there left suddenly so all their belongings remained. It seemed so strange to me, like a nuclear bomb warning had gone off and everyone had dropped everything and gone to the bomb shelter. Yvan led me up the stairs, and I listened as his shoes thudded heavily against the steps. He didn't look like a priest in his close-fitting white T-shirt, blue jeans, and brogues. I'd heard the tap of his brogues on the concrete as he'd feinted here and there, and I pictured the warm brown tips of the brogues peaking out from under Yvan's bed in his room. That was where he put them when he unshod his feet. Yvan led me to a bedroom and we sat on the edges of the metal frame since the mattress had been removed. Yvan told me that this was where he went when he needed to be alone. Paul had the fairgrounds and Yvan had his abandoned house. No one ever came here because it was close to the shut-down mill where heroin addicts shot themselves up.

"Do you like Paul?" Yvan asked me.

I told him that I couldn't like Paul in the way that he meant. How could I? "But we're still people even though we're in the seminary. We're not robots," he said. I told Yvan that I knew we weren't robots, but that didn't change how I felt about Paul. I couldn't see him in a romantic way. Then Yvan told me that he hadn't liked boxing all that much even though he'd been good at it. Maybe he liked it at first, but after a while he'd grown to hate it. That's how things are in life: you like them at first and then you grow to hate them. We turned to the sound of teenagers laughing and roughhousing loudly down the street. Yvan told me that boxing had been sweet at first, but then it wasn't sweet anymore.

3

AUGUST 8, 2008

From the window Yvan could see the forest that surrounded the house and the canal that ran all the way to the closed-up mill. In the coming days I'd hear the phantom thuds of the workers' boots as they journeyed to work in the early hours and as they trudged home when their shifts were done. As I sat in my bedroom in the rooming house after that night with Yvan, I thought about how different he was from Paul. Before me I saw Yvan's fawn-brown hair, his hairless face, his broken nose and his defeated look, just as if he had been standing in the room with me. Yvan had never lost a match in his amateur career and his friend Maxime described him to me later as an automaton of jabs and feints, but somehow Yvan was still defeated. He was like someone who'd been born knowing that a terrible fate awaited them, it was only a matter of time. I spoke to Paul the next day, and he wasn't mad that I'd left St. Vincent's with Yvan. I never saw Paul mad about anything. Whenever things took a turn in life, he just grabbed a hold of his shiny, silver belt buckle and laughed it off. I imagined Paul holding his belt buckle and laughing that way as I spoke on the phone with him talking about that night at St. Vincent's. Paul wanted to hang out again, and when the fairgrounds reopened for the carnival, he called me to suggest that I go there with him and Yvan to see how the place looked when it was open. We didn't get to see the funhouse as it was closed for renovations, though that was the thing I was most curious about. I wanted to know what it looked like inside the devil's mouth.

Yvan drove me home that night too. He got out of the car to walk me to my door, and after he'd returned to the car and had driven off, I glanced up to see the landlady watching me from the window. As soon as she realized I'd seen her, she quickly pulled the gauzy curtain closed, but it was a silly thing to do since I could still make out her portly shape behind the fabric. She was waiting for me on the mid-stairs when I unlocked the front door and entered the house. "He's very handsome," she said, but it was just another one of her accusations. *How dare you bring such a handsome thing home when you know I'm alone and lonely,* she might have said. *You're just an out-of-town whore with a butter-wouldn't melt face.* She had turned and walked up the stairs before I could say anything to her in response.

"Hail Mary full of grace. Blessed art thou amongst women," prayed the landlady in her bedroom as I stood at the door and waited for her.

When she saw me, she said: "Oh, Charlotte, I wanted to talk to you," and then she informed me that she thought I ought to move someplace else as she didn't think having such a young woman here was a good idea after all. Most of the other tenants were men, and she seemed to prefer that arrangement. She stood up and walked to her dresser to show me listings she'd found in the newspaper of other places in town that were renting, and in the process she knocked over the toy soldiers that she'd had sitting atop the dresser. I didn't need to leave that very day, only within 30 days, and I wasn't worried about finding another place as I had already spoken to Paul that morning about a building in town that he'd passed that he thought would be perfect for me. I didn't tell the landlady that.

I left her house two weeks after I went out with Paul and Yvan, and I'd only been in the new apartment for a few days when Yvan stopped by. The apartment was a real one this time with its own bathroom and a balcony, not simply a room in someone else's house. Paul had offered to help me move, but I wanted to do everything on my own so I didn't call him when the time had come. I had previously bought a table and chairs, which I'd have to bring with me in the move, but I still didn't call him. I only called Paul after I was already settled. We promised to arrange a time to meet for a housewarming, but we never did. Yvan came instead. It was early evening and I'd just returned to the apartment from the diner where I worked. The diner hadn't been busy so the pinafore the waitresses were made to wear was still pearly white, aside from a couple barely-there grease stains.

In the process of cleaning dishes I'd left in the sink, I knocked over a mug in the shape of bear. And then in my haste to pick up the pieces I pricked my finger. After throwing the fragments of the mug into the trash, I glanced at my pricked and swollen finger and told myself that I should never have bought that bear mug at all. I'd bought it the same day that I'd moved into the apartment after seeing it in a shop window. I made dinner, and what I didn't finish I placed in Tupperware. Tupperware of Rubbermaid, I didn't know the difference. I sat down and thought to myself how nice it would be to see Yvan again, even though he was studying at the seminary. I liked to picture myself in the company of other people when I was alone, and for the past weeks I'd begun to picture myself with Yvan. Nothing specific, we were just walking together. We walked down the street as the millworkers went to the mill or returned from it, or as the Amish man delivered his goods to the grocery store in his horse and buggy. I remembered Yvan's hands, which were tanned and angrily calloused, and I turned to the sound of a lark fluttering to the window and landing on the windowsill. I learned later that these frequent guests were Western meadowlarks, which are not true larks. I hadn't been pondering the lark long when I heard a knock at the door. The knock surprised me as I hadn't had any visitors since I'd moved here. Opening the door, I was met with Yvan's familiar face.

"How'd you get into the building?" I asked him.

"Don't be mad," Yvan said. "Paul told me that you'd moved and I thought I'd drop by. I bought a house-warming gift."

Yvan reached into a paper bag he held and produced the smallest pair of lilies I'd ever seen, but it was nice. I told Yvan to come in and led him to the table where I'd been sitting before. We exchanged the niceties of people who don't know each other well because it was as if we were meeting one another again. I'd only seen Yvan twice. Yvan made a joke about how sparsely furnished my apartment was and I laughed though I was somewhat annoyed by that comment. I also believed my apartment needed furnishing so it was like a wayward arrow had unexpectedly hit its mark. As Yvan was replying to a remark I made about how frustrating it can be to acquire and move furniture when you live in a walk-up apartment, I remembered that I was still wearing my pinafore from work, which I then made haste to remove. The owner of the diner liked the waitresses to wear pinafores over their dresses because he had a French maid fetish. We didn't really look like French maids though. Perhaps we did to a man that had a fetish.

"I forgot I was still wearing that," I said when I returned to the living room from the kitchen where I'd gone to place the pinafore.

"Is that for work?" Yvan asked.

"Yeah," I said. "Not many people these days where those at home."

"Oh, I don't know. I actually wanted to talk to you about something else."

"What?" I asked, and I sat down across from Yvan at the boxy table that was squashed against a living room wall since I didn't have a dining room. Yvan looked very athletic in his khakis, and I again made a note about how he stood apart from the other seminarians I'd met. He told me that he was a first-year at the seminary school, which I already knew since Paul had told me, and he said that he'd probably be done with his education in another three years, maybe four.

I said: "When you get your own church, you'll be very popular with the church ladies."

Yvan didn't understand at first because he was like that. It was like a part of him didn't understand that opportunistic side of people. Yvan's khakis had frayed edges like when a boy has worn them too long and a thread eventually comes loose and gets caught in the mechanism of the clothes dryer. Though Yvan was being perfectly respectable, a surprising degree of familiarity seemed to have formed between us because we were attracted to one another. Yvan's eyes lingered too long on me when I spoke, and I'm sure that the same was true of me when he spoke. He told me that he was doing poorly in French, and I said he was in luck since I'd graduated with a master's in French. He was too polite to ask why someone with a master's in French was working at the diner, so it was nice not to have to answer that. I thought he'd ask about my family as Paul had done and that I'd have to explain all that again, but he didn't. Boxer he may be, but Yvan understood the politeness of not asking a new acquaintance too many personal questions.

"I thought you might want to tutor me," Yvan finally said.

I told Yvan that I needed to check my calendar since the coming week looked full, which wasn't true. That's when he told me I was unlikely to find any students to tutor in this anti-intellectual town. I laughed and asked Yvan if he wanted to stay to share a batch of brownies that I'd bought. Yvan had a special affection for brownies, which Sherry interrupted the story to confirm. Even she remembered Yvan's sweet tooth. He told me he'd be happy to stay if we were having brownies. I found the box of brownies and decided to serve along with the brownies two cups of hot chocolate with marshmallows. Making the hot chocolate meant we had to wait for the kettle to be brought to a boil, and when it had I had to take the piping kettle off the stove and pour the boiled water into cups. Then I

would dump the contents of two hot chocolate pack-
ets into two separate cups. After I did that, I returned
to the humble table where Yvan sat.

Yvan asked me if I'd been to the camera shop
around the corner, which the town evidently was
famous for. Well, that and all the closed-down lumber
mills. I told him that I hadn't, and he tapped his foot
as he finished off the last of the brownies. "I wish I
had more, but that was the last one," I told him. Yvan
became more at ease, which I discerned by his taking
off his jacket, the same leather jacket he had draped
over my shoulders before. I told Yvan that he was
right, that I was having difficulty finding students to
tutor, and that I'd be happy to take him on as a student. I mentioned that he'd have to compensate me
for my time.

"Of course, I'd pay you," Yvan said. "I'm not a thief."

"A thief?"

"You know what I mean. I'm not someone who
skips out on paying people."

"Are your professors all priests?" I asked.

"Most of them. Not all," said Yvan.

"That's nice."

"No, it's not."

"No, I meant that you occasionally get someone to
teach you who's not from the priesthood."

"Right. And if I fail French, I can just leave the
seminary and get a job," but I didn't think Yvan meant
that to be taken seriously.

"I don't want to go back to boxing, but I guess I could go back to that if I really can't find anything to do."

"You still look like a boxer."

"Do I?"

"You do."

"I don't know how I feel about you living alone here," Yvan said, looking sheepishly around the narrow confines of the apartment. "You don't know many people in town and it's not safe."

"It's not like I moved to an island of cannibals," I said. "I'm sure I'll be fine."

"But you don't know anyone but Paul and me."

"I know," I said.

"I'm really glad I met you, Charlotte," said Yvan, standing up.

I glanced up at him, and he added: "Now I have someone to tutor me in French. I'm set."

Yvan left, promising to call, and I took a shower as I'd intended to do when I returned home from the diner. The walls in the apartment were thin, and I could hear the tenants in the neighboring apartments slamming their doors and walking in and out of rooms. I heard people marching up and down the stairs or arguing loudly with one another through the walls. When I stepped out of the shower, I dried myself with a towel and stepped toweled into the living room where I passed my fingers over the lilies that Yvan had bought. They sat in a pot of gruesome black plastic. Picking up the remote control, I sat at the table and turned on the television. I watched a TV movie about a woman who gets a present of lilies from a man that she's just met. She's been following him for a long time, but he doesn't know it. I had to watch the standard channels as I didn't have cable. It was after 10PM when I heard a knock at the door. I dressed myself hurriedly and answered it.

"I'm Mary," the woman in the hall said. "I live next door."

"Right, I've seen you before."

"Sorry to bother you, but I thought I heard your television going and I just wanted to warn you not to watch the documentary about Jack the Ripper since it's right before bedtime. Jack did some really gory stuff to people and you might have nightmares."

I laughed in a friendly way and promised not to watch anything having to do with Jack the Ripper.

The next day, I sat by the phone waiting for Yvan to call as he'd told me that he would phone me to schedule our first session. I didn't have a shift at the diner that day. Yvan called me shortly after I'd put the remainder of lunch in Tupperware and done the dishes. He suggested we could have our first session that night, though it might be a challenge for me as we hadn't discussed at length what he already knew. I told Yvan that I wasn't an amateur and I'd be able to determine the appropriate course of study based on his level of language understanding.

Our first lesson passed without incident, though there was some strangeness having to do with him studying to be a priest and being tutored by me in my apartment. We both felt it. Before the session was over, we agreed that there wasn't enough space for tutoring there and we'd have to arrange to meet someplace else. As Yvan was leaving he invited me to a get-together at the house of Maxime, who was another seminary student. Maxime actually lived across the street from me, Yvan told me, though I'd never met him before. Like Yvan and Paul and many of the other residents of the mill town, Maxime was descended from French-Canadians that had moved to the area over the last seventy years. They'd been poor when they'd come, but most were less poor now. And Maxime's family weren't poor at all. I thought it was strange that Yvan's parents were French-Canadians, but he couldn't understand French.

A few hours after Yvan left, Paul stopped by. I hadn't seen Paul in weeks and I'd almost forgotten about him. It was as if he'd been completely displaced from my memory by Yvan. Paul also brought a house-warming gift: two dozen yellow roses in a glass vase. I set them on the table in the living room as Paul glanced around the apartment. I suggested Paul follow me to the kitchen so I could pour him a glass of water.

After his first sip from his glass, Paul said: "Yvan

told me he stopped by today. I wondered why you had invited him and not me."

"I didn't invite him," I told Paul. "He just stopped by on his own. He said you told him where I lived."

"Oh. Yeah, that's true. I guess I did. I didn't think he'd drop by though. You're tutoring him now?"

"Yes, I am."

"He's not stupid, Charlotte," said Paul.

"I never said that he was. And I don't think he's stupid either."

"He's a townie. From this town I mean. We both are," said Paul. "I don't think the priesthood means the same thing to him as it does to me. I don't know what it means to him, but I know I want to be a priest. I can minister to people's spiritual needs and I won't have to live in this town forever. There's something about being a priest that seems right to me and I'm fascinated by all the saints. Their lives. Their names. Saint Odile, ever heard of her?"

"No."

"Oh, she's cool. If you pray to her, she could cure your blindness. It only helps if your blind though."

"That's nice."

"And if you become a priest, you can be sent any-where in the world. Even Australia or Argentina."

Paul told me that his father had been a felon who'd gotten rich by opening a chain of car dealerships after he'd gotten out of prison. It was the last thing I'd ever expect someone like Paul to stay and I was taken aback, so I just sat quietly watching him. Paul asked me if the lilies on the table were from Yvan and I told him that they were. His large hands rubbed the long petals of the flowers.

"Yvan has a cousin Jacques who became a pilot, and Yvan's brother, well, you'll see when you meet him," said Paul. "If you do."

"Maybe I will. Yvan never mentioned it."

"Do you like him?"

"Who?"

"Yvan."

"I don't know what you mean," I remarked.

"I mean do you like him in a physical way," said Paul.

"No," I told Paul. "I don't like him in a physical way, as you put it. And I don't know why you would even ask me that."

"You don't think he's handsome?"

"He's attractive, but I don't see what that has to do with anything. He's my student."

"Is that what he is?" Paul asked, but it wasn't really a question. He was kind of smirking.

"I don't know what I did to make you angry, Paul," I said.

"You haven't made me angry, Charlotte," said Paul. "I was just curious about a few things."

"I hope your curiosity doesn't put us off being friends," I said. "I hope that we can always be friends."

"I hope so too," said Paul, though we both understood that any passing friendship we'd initiated had already ended.

"You don't think Yvan's different from the other seminary students?" Paul asked.

"I do think he's different, but I wouldn't really know, would I?"

"No. I never asked how old you were."

"26."

Paul left after that. It was still early, but I readied myself for the party at Maxime's house. I found a shop nearby: a rundown place dwarfed by the red brick buildings around it. I changed into a little black dress in the changing room and marched straight to the party. My old clothes I stuffed into my purse. I wasn't wearing any panties. It surprised me how self-conscious I'd become because I knew Yvan would be there, but Sherry said she understood. She wanted another cup of tea so she walked into the kitchen in her trailer and put a kettle on the stove.

I met Yvan outside my apartment and we laughed as he pointed across the street to Maxime's house. It was a two and a half story directly across the street from the First National Bank, and when Yvan crossed the street to reach it I followed. He was wearing his brogues again and they made a dull tap on the asphalt. The front door to Maxime's house was unlocked and there were all sorts of shady people congregated on the porch. There were even more in the front hall of the house, which had a sweeping stair going up to

33

the second floor. It was a nice house if you pictured it without all the people in it. It had parquet floors and crown molding. The ceiling was high and the walls were wainscoted. A woman bumped into me as I followed Yvan into the house, and when she realized what she'd done she turned around and apologized. I was surprised to see women there.

I was surprised at how comfortable Yvan was with these people that all seemed to have something irreligious about them, but then I remembered that Yvan hadn't always wanted to be a priest. I pictured him shadow boxing with himself on the night we'd met. The image of his lithe, masculine shadow on the pavement joined by that of the Amish man and his horses would linger. Yvan's shadow was not nearly as lithe and sensual as he was in life. Maxime didn't appear immediately, but he would soon enough. He shared the house with his friends, only some of whom were in the seminary. The music boomed, but it seemed to drop to silence as we maneuvered about the house because I was concentrating on Yvan who led me and what we might say to one another if we were alone. After a short conversation with someone he knew, Yvan led me past a gyrating young woman and a banjo leaning against the wall into the kitchen. One of Maxime's roommates was baking gingerbread men. A man who looked like a seminarian opened the refrigerator to remove a bottled water, and I smiled at the spicy scent in the air from the cookies. The person who'd cooked them had put too much ginger in them.

A girl was hiding in the pantry and she appeared shortly after Yvan left the kitchen. Someone in the living room had called Yvan's name so he left. The girl from the pantry introduced herself and explained that she didn't live there, she was just friends with some of the guys. "Why would someone want to live with seminary students?" she asked, but I don't know what she meant by that. She wore a dress that looked like a cheerleading outfit, like she was going to a horror-themed costume party. Most of her supple thighs were visible. She incessantly moved her hair from one side of her neck to the other like some people do, but she was pretty. She said that she had dated one of the guys that lived in the house, so they weren't all seminarians after all. There was another girl in the kitchen washing dishes and looking out the window. At one point she said: "My father owns three acres outside of town and keeps some chickens, but I told him he should sell the house because it's falling apart." I didn't know who she was talking to until I saw the tall man in blue jeans leaning against the wall.

Maxime showed up just as the girl by the sink was taking the gingerbread men out of the oven. She spent so much time talking and listening to people that I was sure she'd burn them. "What are you doing in here with these skanks?" Maxime asked me, and the girl gasped. I told Maxime playfully that he shouldn't say things like that, but really I was surprised that he knew who I was as I'd never met him before. He'd spoken to me like he knew me. "I didn't mean anything by it," Maxime said, playfully patting me on the hand. He introduced himself, actually spending a lot of time describing himself and his situation, and that gave me a chance to get a good look at him. He was about average height and had an insinuating quality. His face was rough and prematurely-aged, and he had wing-shaped eyebrows. But he had an athletic build, tending more towards thinness than Paul and Yvan. His hair was dark brown, nearly black, and slightly curly. When Maxime led me out of the kitchen, which he insisted upon, I asked him why he didn't like those other girls, and he told me that he didn't dislike them. It was just a joke. It was a party after all.

"I don't have to live here if I don't want to," he said. "I just couldn't get into the dorm at the seminary and I don't want to live alone. I'm actually renting the whole house and subletting it to these other people."

"Why couldn't you get into the dorm?" I asked.

"I got in off the wait list," said Maxime. "Yes, they even have wait lists at seminaries. The issue was that I decided at the last minute to apply to the school. And then it took me forever to get all the shit they wanted. References and letters from people that I had volunteered with. Shit like that."

We had stopped in the hall because of a glut of revelers hanging about, and Maxime leaned against the wall towards me, sort of pinning me against it. Then he laughed and we kept walking. That's when we met another one of Maxime's roommates who looked me up and down in a very unfriendly way. He was tall and looked less like a priest than even Maxime. His look was fierce and I thought his hair was overly-styled for a seminary student. After examining me for a while he said: "I know who you are. You're that bitch who slept with Tommy. You got him kicked out of school. That's what you do, you sleep with guys studying for the priesthood and get them kicked out of seminary school. Janice, right? You're the one that slept with Tommy."

Maxime pulled me away and said: "Don't worry about him. He's crazy. We've got a few really crazy guys at the seminary. He thinks most of the girls that come here are sleeping with Tommy."

"Who's Tommy?"

"He's this guy who got kicked out last year. I don't really know him because this is my first year, but I've seen him before. He's trying to get back in. And this other guy, yeah, forget about him. He's on medication. Whether he takes the medication or not is a different story. Don't pay any attention to him. You're very pretty and pretty people naturally attract a fair amount of shit. And Yvan told me about St. Vincent's."

St. Vincent's seemed like years ago, and I told Maxime so.

"Are you having a good time?" Maxime asked.

"At the party? I think so," I said.

Maxime led me upstairs and it was suddenly quiet. The music still blared, but because we weren't crammed in with all the other people it seemed like there wasn't any music at all. There were several bedrooms on the second floor. As we passed the first room, I looked in and saw that one man was changing his clothes and the other man was fiddling with a radio antenna. We passed a second room where two women were chatting about a young man that they'd seen downstairs and were both attracted to. We eventually came to Maxime's room, which was at the end of the hall. I was surprised that it was smaller than the other rooms since he said he was the one renting the house.

"I don't think you're supposed to have girls in your rooms," I said as I followed Maxime in.

"That's a pretty dress," said Maxime.

"No, I said I don't think you're supposed to have girls in your rooms."

"I heard you. We're not supposed to have girls in our rooms when we're on campus, but I'm not on campus, am I? I'm in this kind of limbo since I'm supposed to be on campus as a first-year, but I'm not so they can't tell me shit. Not here."

I walked to the window, passing the Singer sewing machine and the hatbox. There was an electric fan rattling on top of the bureau. The fan was switched on even though it had suddenly grown cold in the town, and the air circulated by the fan shook the paper-thin curtains. I saw that Maxime's window looked out onto the street, and on the far side of the street sat the bank and the entrance into my apartment building. The window to my own apartment was above somewhere. On a table beside his bed Maxime had a hatbox, which he opened as he sat in the bed. It was an antique hatbox filled with important papers and photographs. Maxime showed me a picture of him in his hockey uniform from college and another picture of him and Yvan when they'd gone swimming in the lake. It seemed like Maxime and Yvan had gone to school together. Yvan was smiling in the picture, and it occurred to me that I'd never seen him smile before. At least not in that happy and free way that men have when they're only around their male friends. Yvan was shirtless and more formidable than you'd expect a boxer to be. Yvan dwarfed Maxime, who was also shirtless, but who had the thin musculature of a diver or a featherweight boxer. Then Maxime showed me another picture of him and Yvan and a third person named Fritz. I never discovered who this Fritz was. Perhaps that wasn't his name and Maxime made it up.

Maxime told me that he was happy that I was tutoring Yvan, but he didn't say why precisely. He said that we should go out for a drive some time because even though the town was grim and oppressive with its half-shut strip malls and closed mills, there was some woods surrounding the town that were worth seeing, which I already knew as I'd seen them. When you maneuvered about the town, the smokestack from the lone remaining mill outside of town depressed you since you knew the millworkers were trudging there and would be out of work when the mill owners finally closed that mill like all the others. As I stood there by the window, I forgot about Maxime who was droning on about something. At one point, Maxime stood up and approached me slowly. He glanced at me with a serious expression and reached a hand slowly toward my face. He brushed the hair away from my brow with his hand and left a hand possessively on the back of my neck. I pulled his hand down. When I left the room, I didn't say anything. I turned around before I walked out completely, and I saw that Maxime was watching me closely. "There's plenty of girls like you in this town," he said. "You're nothing special." I left the upper floor and found Yvan standing in the foyer. I had to stop myself from hugging him. He told me that he'd been looking for me, but he hadn't been able to find me since he didn't know where I'd gone to. He'd even searched outside. I compared Yvan standing there in the foyer to how he looked in Maxime's pictures, and it occurred to me that Yvan was gradually emerging from his chrysalis. Yvan was in the process of turning into something other than the boxer he'd been, while Maxime was in a state of unbecoming or never becoming.

4

AUGUST 30, 2008

During my first tutoring session with Yvan, I noticed that he had a scar above his right eye. He told me that he'd gotten into a fight with his father and that he'd sliced him with a letter opener. I only saw the scar because the table lamps they have in the study rooms at the seminary shine this blinding light right into your face. Yvan's eyes were trusting and frank. He had a look of clueless faith in his eyes, and I wondered if he'd looked at other boxers that way when he fought. It didn't seem to me that he could trust them. We'd talk about all sorts of things during our sessions. We'd just wander from one topic to the next, which was easy because Yvan had a mind that floated along like a maple leaf drifting in the air, at least when he spoke and said the things he wanted to. Sometimes people edit themselves. We started talking about how I used to watch the men in hunting gear driving in their jeeps from the diner window. Yvan said those men better hope that deer don't make guns of their own one day and turn the tables.

"They might do the same to us if they could," he said. "Skin us and eat us."

That's what animals do. They turn on one another and you can never trust them. Yvan told me that when the monks were founding the monastery that the seminary would later be attached to, they asked for a series of ridiculous things. At least they seemed ridiculous to Yvan. They wanted dressed fox-skins since the woods around the town teemed with silver foxes, and they wanted a relic. Every good monastery needed a relic so visitors would come. Yvan said the monks were sent the femur of a French saint that no one was quite sure had ever existed. His name was invoked to protect people from succubi.

I worked at the diner some days and tutored Yvan on others, but there were many days that I was free. I told Sherry that it was on one of my free days that I got to know Shannon, one of my neighbors in the apartment building I'd moved to. But meeting Shannon started first with Luc, who was the first neighbor that I'd met. One morning I heard a knock at the door as I was cleaning out the refrigerator, and I suspected it was Luc. It was, and he asked me if I wanted to come over to his place for breakfast. I didn't really but I was curious about whether he was a fair cook or not.

He was. He made a savory breakfast of over-easy eggs, ham, sausage, and Canadian bacon all while dancing to the music on the radio. I didn't want to laugh at him but there was something so free and foreign about his mannerisms that I couldn't help it. It reminded me of this French film I saw where these two young French-men were singing a silly, old-fashioned song as they were walking home at midnight arm in arm. Luc told me that he was friends with the butcher and bought all his meat there instead of at the supermarket.

"Why buy meat pumped with preservatives if you can get the real thing," he told me. "We live practically in the woods. You can get anything out there."

We sat across from one another at the kitchen table: him in his ribbed, sleeveless shirt, and I in my silk blouse and blue jeans. I was feeling confident that day and I think I might have tolerated Luc's compliments about my appearance, but none were forthcoming. He told me that he'd always wanted to go to the Holy Land to view the sights, but he didn't think he'd ever have the chance because of all the bad dreams he'd been having.

"What kind of dreams?" I asked.

"Oh, all sorts of things," said Luc. "I dreamt that a boy came here and was showing naughty pictures of women. Like those pinup pictures from the '50s and '60s. You've probably seen them in the movies."

"Yeah. I'm sure I have. I wonder why he did that, that boy in your dream."

"I don't know. Sometimes you wake up in the middle of a dream and you don't get to see how it ends. Or the dream just cuts to a different scene like in the movies or a TV show. I had a dream with you in it, you know."

"What was I doing?"

"Oh, you must have met some guy in a bar or something because you went back to his place outside of town," said Luc. "It was this old place with buck heads mounted on the walls and wood paneling everywhere. There was a fireplace. You were making out with him."

"And on that note, I think I'll be off," I said.

I laughed nervously as I got up from where I'd been sitting and Luc said: "Goodbye, Charlotte. I hope you enjoyed your breakfast."

"I did, thank you. I can help with the dishes if you'd like."

"No, you don't have to," said Luc. "Actually, I'd rather do them myself. You just go on with your day and I'll see you another time. Going shopping again?"

"Oh, no," I replied. "I think I've spent double my allotment for the month."

But it wasn't true because I had only been in my apartment five minutes when I decided to go out, purely out of restlessness. The store I went to was practically empty as it was early morning, and the shop assistants were all sitting around reading books or magazines. I walked up to a dark-haired woman who was sitting by the window with her back resting against the glass, and I asked her if she knew where the socks were as I couldn't find them. She gave me a long look, not mean, but long. She was pretty and her perfume was so strong that I smelled it as soon as I walked into the store.

"You don't recognize me, do you?" she asked.

"Should I?"

"Shannon," she said. "I live in your apartment building."

"You do?"

"You probably haven't seen me before."

"No, I'm sure I have. There's just been so much going on that I'm a little scatterbrained. It's early too and I haven't had my coffee yet."

"No, it's fine. I've been meaning to invite you over to meet you officially. Do you have a boyfriend?"

"I don't," I said.

"Well, that's good. What kind of coffee do you drink?" asked Shannon. "I get off at two, but I have to make a grocery run. I guess I'll be home by three. I'm in 3F, sort of across from you and down the hall a little bit. Close to the stairs. Well, closer to the stairs than you. It would be nice if you could drop by. I'll make lunch and put on a nice pot of coffee. Don't look that way. I'm not a serial killer, I promise. We actually get really good coffee up here, although the nice stuff can get very expensive."

"Why did you make that comment about being a serial killer?" I asked Shannon later in her apartment.

She was in the kitchen, but I could hear her laughter from where I sat in the living room. Her apartment was much larger than mine or Luc's. She told me later that it had once been two apartments that a rich widow had combined. Shannon had two large bedrooms though she lived there herself.

"I write to a serial killer who lives nearby and I guess it was just on my mind," said Shannon from the kitchen.

"You're joking," I said.

"No, I'm not. Rutherford Tracy. He's on death row for assaulting and murdering 15 men in Gary, Indiana 14 years ago. Well, he's been on death row for 14 years. The rapes and murders happened over several years. His case is in appeal."

"Oh my God, Shannon. Why?"

Shannon peaked her head through the kitchen doorway, and when I turned to glance at her she was smiling. The walls were painted a very lively baby blue, and the blue of the walls matched the several blue ribbons Shannon had tied in her full, dark hair.

"It started out as a school project," she said. "I went to community college to study accounting, but then I switched to criminal justice. I finished my degree, the two-year degree, but I never went on to a four-year school like they wanted me to. I decided I didn't want anything to do with law enforcement. I suppose I wrote Tracy because I thought he was interesting and I was curious if he really had a personality disorder like all the FBI investigators were saying. I'm surprised you haven't heard of him."

"I'm sure I have," I said. "Maybe I just forgot."

"He's famous. I guess the reason why I wrote him was because I saw his picture in the paper once when his case was coming up for appeal, and there was just something interesting about him. I won't say he's handsome because he's not, but he's a bulky, masculine guy. And I guess that's attractive to some people. He was just so interesting to me and I didn't want to write my paper on someone boring. I thought it would be incredible if I could actually get him to write me back. I didn't think he would."

I stood up and was walking around Shannon's living room. There were framed pictures of herself with her friends, but I mostly admired her equestrian paintings. My father had taken me to horseracing events when I was younger, and I had always wanted an apartment filled with paintings of horses. Beside one of the paintings was a photograph of Shannon herself astride a large horse that looked like a Clydesdale or a Percheron: a working horse that you don't commonly see around. Shannon's shapely body was apparent astride the horse. She had a modern dancer's body and wore very feminine boots that came all the way up to the knee.

"I made a dark roast," Shannon shouted from the kitchen. "I hope you don't mind."

"What?"

"I said that I made a dark roast. I hope you don't mind."

"No, that's fine," I said. "I was just admiring your art here."

"It's a bit much for a small apartment," Shannon said, returning with our coffee. "I have a friend who makes reproductions and that's what these are. Reproductions."

"This isn't a small apartment," I told her. "You should see mine."

"No, I can imagine," said Shannon. "It's a pre-war building, and I can see you sleeping in the typical bachelor one bedroom. About 350 square feet?"

"That sounds about right."

"Do you like living here?"

"In this building?"

"No," said Shannon. "In town."

"I don't mind. My aunt used to live in a border town like this when I was little. Sort of a mill town, I guess, with a lot of French-Canadian people. Or at least French names and surnames. No, it's quaint. There's a lot of character here, and to me it seems familiar."

"That's nice," Shannon said. "No one wants to live someplace that's uncomfortable. Tracy says you should change your locale once in a while to someplace unfamiliar, but it's nice that it already feels like home to you."

"What's he like?"

"Tracy? He's very polite and intelligent. And he has a very deep, manly voice. Like really butch."

"You've spoken to him on the phone?"

"Of course," said Shannon. "It started out with letters, but we speak all the time on the phone now." And after a pause: "You never told me what you do for a living?"

"I'm working at a diner, but really I want to teach. I'm tutoring a seminary student right now."

"I see," said Shannon. "I'm not really from this town either. I was married before and my husband was from here, so that's why we moved here. He worked at the mill. Actually, he was the manager at the mill before he left to do something else. It's a long story. Anyway, I'll just say that he wanted me to do things in that marriage that I wasn't willing to do."

"You don't have to say any more than that," I remarked.

"So that's how I ended up in the town, and I don't know if I'll leave anytime soon," said Shannon. "It's decent. There aren't that many truly old buildings in town like I would like. There's something very blank about the town. Even the people can be really blank and faceless. I didn't go to the community college until after I separated. I've been writing Tracy for about two years now."

"His case has been in appeal that long?"

"Yes. The appellate process takes forever. It's funny. I know Tracy is manipulative and that I shouldn't trust him, but when I'm taking to him on the phone, I can feel myself completely giving in to him. He always calls me at night, like really late. Sometimes after midnight. I think he does that on purpose. Maybe he thinks I'm vulnerable then. He knows I'm alone."

I stood up from where I sat at the table and marched over to what I'd decided was my favorite among Shannon's paintings. It was entitled "Brown Horse of the Steppe," which I discerned from some small lettering at the bottom of the canvas, close to the frame. I turned around to see that Shannon was watching me. Her face was serious but mostly like she was waiting for a reaction of some kind out of me. She smoothed a crease in her jeans and took a sip from her coffee.

"What do you mean vulnerable?" I asked her.

"He's not a stupid person, Charlotte," Shannon said. "He knows what to say to people to get them to open up and reveal things about themselves. He knows how to make a certain kind of first impression. And I know he's doing it, but I still can't help myself. I am vulnerable. Anyone would be vulnerable to someone like him. He's predatory. But it's an irresistible kind of thing. You should hear him when he speaks."

"No, I don't want to," I mouthed soundlessly.

I met Yvan at his seminary: passing the young men that were praying at the altar of a chapel to reach the library where Yvan wanted to meet. When I walked into the library, I was met with the thinly-veiled aston-ishment of the young men, though they were swift to politely look away or pretend to be involved in other things, like admiring the sacred tibia or beatified toe imprisoned behind glass display cases. Yvan had told me he'd be up on the second floor and had given me the room number. As I ascended the stairs, the boys treated me like a pariah, moving as far to the other side of the stairs as they could. When I found Yvan, his back was to me and he was taking off his coat. In the process, the ends of his dress shirt pulled out of his pants, revealing an inch or two of the muscles of his lower back. It was hardly anything, but it felt as if a significant, intimate moment had passed between us.

"There you are, Charlotte," said Yvan, turning around then and discovering me.

It was a banal room with white-painted walls, wain-scotting, and the figures of angels and saints in the corners. The faces and bodies of these last were heavy with white paint to match the walls. Yvan and I took places across the large oak table, and between us was a table lamp that we turned on. At the time we began our lesson, we were alone in the large room, but soon other young men came in to study in the room later, sitting at a table far behind Yvan and me. They were boisterous when they came in, and Yvan silenced them with a ferocious look. He was able to channel his former ferocity when he needed to. And he remained physically imposing. As we began our lesson, I passed to Yvan the worksheets that I'd prepared with the passages he was to translate. Yvan laughed as if to say that he'd been expecting as much. When he was done, I reviewed his work. It was riddled with errors, but Yvan had improved from our first day together. In truth, Yvan wasn't particularly interested in learning the language.

"We have to learn the language because the founding monastery was in Switzerland," Yvan said.

"I thought you said the monks came from France," I noted.

"No, the patron saint came from France," said Yvan. "If there ever was a saint."

"I met a woman who said she writes to a serial killer," I told Yvan. "It seems so strange to me."

"Not if she loves him," said Yvan.

We'd been studying for some time, and the room had darkened slowly as night fell, but we still had the light from our table lamp. The young men at the other tables had turned on their table lamps too.

"But she doesn't know him" I told Yvan. "She's never met him. She's only written him letters and spoken to him on the phone."

"How many letters has she written?"

"I don't know. Probably dozens, maybe more. They've been writing each other for two years."

"So she's one of those," said Yvan, suppressing a laugh. "One of those women who writes men they know will never get out."

"I don't think it's like that," I remarked. "His case is coming up for appeal. Maybe they'll unearth something, some mistake made by the police, and he'll get out on a technicality."

"Maybe so," said Yvan. "Life isn't fair."

"That doesn't sound like something a priest would say," I said. "Shouldn't you say that God watches everything we do and everything works out the way it's supposed to? That our reward is waiting for us in heaven or some other nonsense."

"Well, I was a boxer before I was priest. And it seems to me that that kind of talk would be lost on you anyway."

I laughed first and Yvan followed. I don't know why we laughed then.

"Maybe I can use this language after all," Yvan continued. "I have a cousin who's a pilot. Jacques. Maybe I'll learn to fly planes and fly myself wherever I want as a missionary."

"That sounds nice."

"It sounds dangerous," said Yvan.

"I still don't understand how you can say Shannon loves Tracy when she doesn't even know him," I remarked as I flipped through the pages of my intermediate French textbook.

"You don't mean Rutherford Tracy from Gary, Indiana?"

"You've heard of him then."

"You haven't?" Yvan asked. "He's famous. He raped and murdered 15 men, and big, strapping guys too."

"I don't want to know," I said.

"Love is a strange thing," said Yvan.

"What do you mean?" I asked.

"And God so loved the world that he gave his only begotten son," said Yvan.

I returned to my apartment and opened a box of breakfast cereal, as I hadn't eaten since I'd been at Shannon's. On the front of the cereal box was the image of a cartoon creature for whom everything in life was simple and straightforward. When you were hungry, you ate. When you wanted to watch television, you turned on the television. I was returning the cereal box to the kitchen cabinet when I heard shouts coming from the hall of the apartment building. I knew they were coming from outside of Shannon's apartment. There's this thing that shouting people do where they don't pause to listen to the other person but continue holding up their end of the shouting battle. Perhaps they reach an impasse where they just have to keep going.

I still wore my shoes, and I opened the door again and left the apartment. It was only after I heard what sounded like a slap that I decided to leave. But before I did, I ran into the kitchen where I grabbed the finished bottle of balsamic vinegar that I'd been planning to recycle. Brandishing the glass bottle, I walked towards Shannon's apartment. I heard another door open in the hall, but I didn't look to see whose door it was. Shannon and her boyfriend continued to yell at one another, and to this was added the cacophony of objects crashing on the hardwood floor. The floors of our old pre-war building were beautiful and not what you would expect in an out of the way mill town like this. I soldiered on to Shannon's door, where I was met by the face of Shannon's boyfriend.

"And you are?" he asked.

"I'm Charlotte. I live across the hall. You should be ashamed of yourself."

The boyfriend laughed, turning his face to one side as some people do.

"All right, Miss. We'll keep our shameful behavior to ourselves. You can go on your way now."

"Charlotte, over here," said a small voice. It was Luc, and he motioned for me to approach his apartment with his hand. "You don't need to get involved in that. Why don't you come in for something to drink?"

Luc held the door open for me. I smelled his cologne and thought it strange that I hadn't noticed it before. It wasn't the cheap cologne that smells good for a few seconds after the man has sprayed it on but is soon gone. I followed Luc to the kitchen table, afraid of what he might say, that I should mind my own business, but he didn't say anything. Luc's long, bushy sideburns were a darker brown than the auburn hair atop his head. You could see a faint line of stubble from where he'd shaved his mustache yesterday. His shoes were old but were in good condition and had been expensive when he'd bought them. At least they looked that way.

"I never told you, but I used to work at the butcher shop," he said.

"Did you?"

"Yes, but then I went to the hospital and the butcher didn't want to hire me back," said Luc. "This was a long time ago, when I was right out of high school."

"You must have hurt yourself at the butcher shop," I said.

"I did, then I completely lost it," said Luc. "I spent the next ten years in and out of psychiatric hospitals. I never went back to work at the butcher's and I never resumed my course at college. I guess that's a regret. Some people think you shouldn't have regrets."

"Not everyone thinks that way," I said. "Most people have regrets."

Luc shrugged his shoulders and looked out the window. Outside, the trees petulantly lashed the windows.

"So that's my story," he said. "What's yours? You haven't told anyone the real reason why you came to town. I'm guessing you were chased out of town after running over a truckload of schoolchildren with your car?"

"No," I laughed.

"You don't have to tell me if you don't want to, Charlotte."

"I'll tell you in my own time," I said. "There may

be a secret, and if there is I'll tell you when the time is right."

In the morning, a child was playing with a toy on a bench facing the apartment building with his mother and curious women leaned out their windows. I could see them from my apartment window. I could also see Maxime's house, and I thought it was odd that I suddenly remembered him then. I had to work that morning, but instead of getting ready I walked to the kitchen and went over all the things I needed to do that week. I was in that state of mind when I heard a knock at the door and whistling coming from behind the door. I opened the door to find Maxime. He was dressed more like a seminarian this time: he wore pleated trousers in a dark color, a black cardigan, and hair somberly parted to one side and gelled.

"I just came from the photography store up the street," he said. "I was getting some pictures developed."

"I didn't know there was a photography store up that way."

"There is. I ran into one of my ex-girlfriends, and it's funny because she kind of reminds me of you. Darker hair, but similar kind of frame. I think you should come out with me and Yvan some time."

"I don't think Yvan has the time," I told Maxime.

5

SEPTEMBER 9, 2008

But Maxime was sure that Yvan had the time, and he wouldn't take no for an answer. I received a phone call soon after from Yvan asking me to join them at a concert. I'd been going through a stack of old mail when he called, and after he hung up I made a pile of the things that I wanted to keep. Topmost among them was a postcard an old friend had sent me from an aviation museum where the planes were so old that they couldn't be flown anymore. I heard the hum of the lawnmower from the superintendent mowing the lawn outside even though my apartment was on the other side of the building. I thought of going to the photography store to get a Canon or a Mamiya so I might take pictures of the superintendent mowing the lawn or of the nosy women leaning out of the windows because they had nothing better to do with their time and didn't know how to mind their own business.

Yvan was the same as ever when I met him at the recital. We agreed to meet there, and I called a cab to drive me. I was early so we sat in back and watched the students and teachers as they arrived and chose their seats. The orchestra scheduled to perform had all traveled together from Europe, and they were busy practicing with their instruments and speaking to one another in an Eastern European language as the guests filed in. There was a hum from the chatter of the attendees arriving and from the instruments. Yvan left our row at one point, and a young-looking student sat on the other side of me with a pair that must have been his parents. There was an excitable woman with dyed auburn hair and a man who looked like he'd rather be on the golf course. The woman said something cheerful and the man muttered something that must have been a remark about how long would they'd have to sit through the concert, though I couldn't hear the words. That's when I heard Maxime say, "Charlotte." When I turned around, I saw him waving at me. He'd run into Yvan and they'd decided to sit somewhere else. I hadn't seen him come in the room, but he was holding fresh-cut lilies. I followed him to a row very close to the orchestra where Yvan, Paul, and a young woman I had never seen before were in the process of taking their seats.

"We came in through a side door," Maxime said, as I sat beside them.

I sat on one side of Yvan while the girl, Joanna, sat on the other side.

"This mist be the warm-up band," said Joanna. "They're not very good."

Yvan laughed, and his laugh was more carefree than I'd ever heard it. It occurred to me that he'd known Joanna a long time.

"I don't think there is a warm-up band," said Yvan. "They just get right into it. But it's from an opera so I guess it sort of builds up."

"Not an opera again," said Maxime. And then he leaned in to whisper to me: "The dean of the school likes operas."

"You should know since you invited us," said Yvan. "Didn't you get a playbill?"

"Yeah, I did actually," said Maxime.

Maxime explained to us that the music was from an opera called *Scheherazade*, which had a famous composition that the dean liked, which is why he'd allowed it to be played even though the subject matter wasn't precisely appropriate. I spent much of the time listening to the chatter of the people sitting behind us rather than to the music. A woman who was a real estate agent explained how she hadn't been selected as Agent of the Month though she deserved it, at least she thought so. The honor had instead gone to a new employee who everyone believed to be romantically involved with one of the partners. The gentleman beside the real estate lady was a stockbroker, and he explained that there wasn't much honor in being Agent of the Year since the recipient didn't get anything other than their name inscribed in a plaque in the office.

Yvan said something and Joanna laughed. I pictured her holding on to Yvan's arm as the crescendo swelled in the musical composition. And the more I thought that way, the more Joanna laughed.

"It's ridiculous," said Maxime, seeming to read my thoughts. "Doesn't she know Yvan's a seminary student and he'll never be able to screw her like she wants?"

"Shut up, Maxime," I whispered.

"It's not the sixteenth century with all the cardinals and bastards and all that," Maxime continued. "Times aren't like that anymore."

"I'm actually enjoying the music."

"Are you? I figured you'd be trying to figure out how close Joanna and Yvan were getting. We can't really see them from where we are."

"I'm not listening to you anymore."

"Jealous?"

"No," I said.

During the intermission, I got a closer look at Joanna and was surprised how pretty she was. She was tall and fair-haired, though her darker roots revealed her natural color. Her eyes were gray-blue and she had very nicely-shaped teeth. Her skirt fell slightly above the knee, and I guessed someone hadn't told her that your skirt should fall below the knee if you're attending a church event, even though we technically weren't in a church. I listened to Joanna tell a story that went every which way in tangents. She said she'd run into her ex-boyfriend at the movie theater, and then after the movie was over he followed her to the parking lot. They had a long conversation about how horribly he had treated her while they were dating. The ex-boyfriend was unapologetic because he wasn't the sort to recognize his mistakes or to apologize if he did. The next day, Joanna was in a rush to run errands before a sociology class and she ended up getting into a car accident. That was her story and the car accident seemed to have nothing to do with the rest of it.

When Yvan took Joanna around to meet one of his seminary students, Maxime said to me: "She's pretty, right?"

"It doesn't matter what I think," I replied.

"Of course, it does."

"You're acting weird tonight," I said. "Actually, you've been acting strangely since I saw you the other day at my apartment. You're different from when I first met you."

"School," said Maxime, suddenly becoming more jocular. "School can drive you insane. You're constantly dealing with guilt. If it's not your guilt, then it's someone else's."

"Then why don't you just quit?"

"Maybe I will."

When the orchestra readied to return to their positions for the end of the intermezzo, Yvan and Joanna came back around again. She seemed to relish being close to Yvan, and I found myself annoyed that Yvan had never officially introduced her to me. And my annoyance about it annoyed me even more. I wondered if I was the insignificant person here, but it didn't matter since Yvan was only a student I was tutoring. He didn't belong to me. Yvan was dapper today. He'd had cut his hair, and although it had been cut a tad too short, the haircut did make him look official: like a new priest arrived to convert an island where they worshiped angry gods. Perhaps they'll eat him, but he still has to look his best. When I asked Maxime why Joanna had told us that story about the car accident she had been in that didn't make any sense, he said that sometimes people relate a story to you, but most of the story is just a distraction from what's really taking place. Maxime said that he wished he'd brought his camera so he could take a picture of all of us together, but he hadn't thought of it.

6

NOVEMBER 9, 2008

Two months later, Maxime did have the chance to take all of our pictures when we met outside of town. Maxime took our picture as the rest of us stood in front of a frozen stream: Yvan, Joanna, Paul and me. He took several pictures, including some in which the girls were encouraged to behave playfully. Just raising their legs into the air and having the boys hold said legs up. Each boy held up a leg and everyone laughed. Maxime was never in any of the pictures because he was always the one holding the camera. It was Maxime's idea that we all go tobogganing, though it had been Yvan who brought Maxime's idea to me. In one of the pictures, the boys were holding the toboggans they'd bought. Since there was one extra boy relative to the girls, Paul would have to go tobogganing alone.

There was an abandoned farm just west of town where woodland sloped down to a creek. There we could hear the birds trilling as they'd yet to migrate elsewhere, and we oft saw their blue wings fluttering across the turnings of the stream. In some places, the stream had halted completely and formed pools, giving the whole area the impression of marshland. Yvan said this was perfect hunting land, although no one hunted here because it was private property. They called the place abandoned, but there had to be a person who owned it somewhere. Perhaps he didn't know he owned it. All I could think was that this sort of place that Rutherford Tracy would bury his bodies: a place where the only inhabitants were the migrating birds and the occasional drug addicts who came here when they had no place to go or forgot where they lived.

Yvan and Maxime selected a hill for us to toboggan down and they brought their pair of toboggans there. No one knew where Paul had gone too. Yvan set his toboggan down, and Maxime told me to get in. I guessed I was to ride down the hill with Yvan. The scene below, with its periodic outcropping of trees and the turning with its seeming veneer of glass, suddenly took on an ominous aspect. I said: "No, I don't want to. We'll hit a tree." Yvan said we wouldn't. He'd sit in front, and I'd sit behind with my arms wrapped around his body. If we did cross paths with a tree, he'd be the one who got the concussion, at least that's how

Yvan presented it to me. We both sat in the toboggan and assumed the positions Yvan had chosen. He
launched the toboggan by first maneuvering it to the
top of the slope. The toboggan surged violently down
the slope, narrowly avoiding colliding with a large tree
branch that we hadn't seen in the sparse light of the
morning. Finally, we landed on a narrow tributary of
the stream.

"We're lucky," I said, noting that the frozen tributary didn't shatter beneath us.

After we got up from the toboggan, being overly
cautious not to crack the ice, Yvan said: "You're looking lovely today."

"You're joking," I said, allowing Yvan to lead me by
the hand to solid ground.

"No, I mean it," said Yvan.

"Now I know you hit your head."

We marched up the hill and waited for Maxime and
Joanna to return. When they did, I said: "All right, now
let's go home."

Maxime said: "What do you think we're jerking off
here? We came here to take the toboggans out, and
we're just getting started. Now we just have to find
someplace else to go, by those trees over there or
behind that house, and we'll find a steeper incline to
sled down."

When Maxime was satisfied that we'd made enough
use of the toboggans, we all got into his car and drove
back to the seminary. We'd found Paul by then. A rail-

way separated the village where we were from the mill town, and we had to wait at the railway crossing as the alarm blared and the barrier came down. As we waited there, I imagined writing a book called "Lost Railways of the US-Canada Border." I'd include a photo of this picturesque railway crossing, picturesque but for its leery aspect and the idea of Shannon's Rutherford Tracy which had followed us from the woods. When we reached the mill town, Maxime drove us to a street I hadn't been down before. He parked the car in the lot of a 24-hour convenience store, and we sat and waited for someone Maxime said would come. "He's coming, just wait," he said. I had a feeling it'd be a drug dealer, and it was. The man Maxime was waiting for came after a 20-minute wait in which I had to endure Joanna and Yvan speaking softly to one another. They spoke in a whispered, seductive Morse code, though I felt Yvan only followed Joanna's lead. She was the offensive fighter here and he only followed her steps in a kind of muted, feckless defense. When Maxime's dealer finally showed, Maxime popped open the car's glove compartment to reveal a wad of cash. Maxime opened the car door and stepped out. He met the dealer in practically the center of the lot, and the rest of us in Maxime's car watched as they exchanged goods.

Joanna said: "I'm scared," and she rubbed a hand across the top of her pink leggings.

Then Yvan said to me, not to Joanna: "Don't worry, Charlotte. It's just pot."

"Thank God," I said.

When Maxime returned to the car, he slammed the car door shut, and we drove on to the seminary. We passed leaning houses hedged in by abandoned buildings with bullet holes in the porch steps. I was surprised to learn that the seminary was only steps away and that the priests from the school performed outreach here. I imagined them surfacing at the school with bloody exit wounds, but Yvan said it wasn't as bad as it looked. Maxime parked the car in a seminary parking lot, and as Yvan and Joanna stepped out Yvan reminded me that we were scheduled to meet the following day for a session.

"You need to drive Charlotte home," Yvan said.

"No, I don't," said Maxime.

"Don't be an asshole. Charlotte lives right across the street from your house so there's no reason not to drive her."

"There's a pretty significant reason not to drive her home, and that's that I'm not going home," said Maxime. "If Charlotte needs to get home, then she could pull up her bootstraps and walk like everyone else."

"Like everyone else? You're in a car, Maxime."

"I'm not driving her."

"It's cold. Just drive her home, asshole."

Maxime drove me home, passing the same oppressive buildings we'd seen on the drive up to the seminary. He didn't reply to my pleasantries when I exited the car. It occurred to me that I needed to go shopping for groceries, so I didn't walk into my apartment building after being dropped off, but instead walked down the street. The nearest grocery store was a short distance away. The store was empty and I was greeted by the checkout girl when I walked in. As I walked the aisles, I noticed how many of the food packages had images of playful animals on them, as if we were all at Disney World and were expected to believe that the world was a happy and small place after all. It may be small, but it's not often happy.

I wasn't in my apartment long because I walked to Shannon's soon afterward. She was holding a cordless phone when she answered the door, and her feet looked petite and feminine in her white socks. "I'm surprised you called, Rutherford," she said. "No, I don't mind that you called collect." Shannon would tell me that inmates always called collect since they weren't allowed money in prison, and if they did have money they couldn't let the prison staff onto it. It was like a whole other world and I was surprised she knew about it. She didn't seem all that different from myself. I followed her to the living room and sat beside her on the couch. She was still talking to Rutherford, and as she did she opened a drawer and showed me all the letters she'd received from him and the negatives of the pictures she'd sent him. I couldn't see them well, but she was in a bra and cutoff jean shorts, displaying her smooth, tanned legs.

"What are you doing?" she asked Rutherford. "You just got out of the shower. God, I can't imagine having to shower with all those guys. I can't imagine what they think about while they're all showering together. Anyway, if you're appeal comes through you won't have to do that for much longer. Yes, Rutherford. My boyfriend knows that I talk to you. I don't know why he let's me. He's crazy. But let's not talk about me. Tell me something I haven't heard before."

I sat there for a while listening to her, and then I walked into the kitchen and poured myself a glass of water. As I drank it, I wondered how I'd feel talking to Rutherford, but I didn't think I could bring myself to do it. I heard a car honk its horn outside, and that brought me away from my thoughts. I poured what was left of the tap water into the sink, I washed the glass, and then I left Shannon's apartment. Shannon laughed as I left, and I turned around to see her stretching her legs out playfully.

"I am definitely not a lesbian!" she shouted happily into the phone.

At home, I tried to follow the workout regimen from the book I'd bought, but I lost interest after about five minutes of wall sits. I'd asked Yvan about it and he told me he'd done it too. Wall sits were a great way to lose weight. I contemplated making dinner, but I wasn't motivated so I went into my bedroom and fell asleep. I had a terrible dream where I opened a letter from the mail and in it was an invitation to a dinner date with Rutherford Tracy at his prison. People I didn't know were standing behind me as I opened the letter and laughing at the seeming inevitability of my predicament. When I awoke, I decided to go to Shannon's. I was still dressed and I thought we'd be able to talk. I slipped into my shoes and left the apartment. I went to Shannon's door and soon realized she wasn't home. I was so adamant on finding her that I began a walking search of the neighborhood. She had to be somewhere. It was after 9PM, and a jaunt to the clothing store where she worked led me to discover that it closed at 7 on weekdays. I continued to walk the streets, trying as best I could to ignore the icy bite from the snow falling. I regretted not having worn boots as my toes in my sneakers began to ache with the cold. But then I saw Shannon. She was sitting in a hole-in-the-wall restaurant and appeared to be waiting for another person.

As soon as I walked in, Shannon noticed me and said unhappily: "What are you doing here, Charlotte?"

"Something happened, Shannon. I just wanted to talk."

"You had a dream about Rutherford, didn't you?" said Shannon. "Was he fucking you?"

"No. My God, how can you even ask that?"

"It's a perfectly logical question. He's a handsome man after all, in his own way."

"I don't know what he looks like, Shannon."
"You didn't look him up on the internet?"
"No."
"Really?
"No, should I?"
"No."

I'd joined Shannon at her booth in the diner, but she was irritated with me and made readiness to leave. She was stopped before she could by a man who joined her on her side of the booth. He introduced himself to me as Spider. Spider and Shannon ordered drinks, and Spider offered to order for me too, but I declined. I told him that I had to work the following day, which wasn't true, but he had no way of knowing whether it was true or not. "So does she," said Spider, pointing to Shannon who shrugged prettily. They both laughed, but Shannon's laughter was guarded. Spider left the booth after he finished his drink. He said he'd be at the bar when Shannon was ready to talk.

"He's a dealer," I told Shannon.

Shannon laughed.

"Really? How do you know that?" she asked.

"Because someone I was with this morning bought pot from him today."

"Funny. He didn't seem to recognize you."

"Because I was sitting in a car and he didn't see me," I told her. "What are you doing?"

"Relax, it's just percocets."

"God, Shannon."

Shannon stood up and I was able to appreciate how attractively her acid-wash jeans hugged her body. "I don't know what to say to you," she said. She told me she'd talk to me later and she joined Spider at the bar. As I wasn't eating, I left the diner, cursing as I was back out in the cold and hadn't had the opportunity to talk in depth about what had happened.

The next day I met Yvan for our scheduled session. I was at the seminary again, waiting for him in the room that had become our regular meeting place. He was late this time and other seminary students began to fill the darkened room, waiting for their study partners. As I waited, I remembered what he'd said about the demands the monks made when they came from Europe and had been asked to found the monastery here. About the fox skins and the other ridiculous things. After some time had passed, I heard the sound of several men chattering in the hall. I knew Yvan was among them, and at least one of the other men sounded like a priest. I had reached the point where I could tell Yvan's voice from the voices of others, easily in fact. Yvan stopped in front of the mouth of the room, and the men with him all took peaks at me in the room. They didn't say anything, and as they walked away their shoes made a happy, confident clack down the hall.

"I'm thinking about taking on another student," I told Yvan.

"But you don't want to," he said.

"Not really, but I will. It's just not enough working at the diner and getting tutoring money from you. I'm sorry."

"It's vulgar to talk about money, Charlotte," Yvan said, but he was laughing.

"Well, some of us have to be vulgar and talk about it."

We both laughed.

"A lot has changed," Yvan says. "You've changed. You're more confident. You seem more at ease. The reality is that I helped you."

"How did you help me?"

"No one would have hired you as a tutor before, Charlotte. These are working class people in this town and they don't like strangers. Besides you look like you have money and they distrust people with money. It's just the way that you dress, Charlotte. You look like a respectable, educated person. You look like someone that a thief would try to rob. You look like you have a summer house on a bay in Massachusetts and all your grandparents went to Harvard or Radcliffe. But now everyone knows that you're tutoring me so it's different. Some people will have seen you at the seminary. You know how women like to talk about everybody. We have female secretaries here, relatives of students. People like that. It may seem minor to you, but you know what people are like. They're looking at you differently. They don't distrust you like they did before. You're like the rest of them now."

"I know how people are, but I don't know how you know," I said.

7

NOVEMBER 13, 2008

I'd come to Shannon's apartment and she was telling me that I shouldn't be so hard on Spider, pouting her lips in the mirror. I didn't really know him, she said. We were sitting in front of the vanity mirror in her bedroom, and she was painting her lips with lipstick. It was a very sultry shade and I wondered where she was going, but she said she was just going back to the diner I'd seen her in the other day to meet a few people. The radio was on, but the reception was poor so our conversation was frequently interrupted by us turning our heads in the direction of the radio static. I told Shannon that I didn't care about Spider, but I didn't think she should get involved with dealers.

"But you don't know him, Charlotte," Shannon said.

"You're right. I don't."

"He's not just a dealer."

When Shannon was satisfied with her appearance in the mirror, she stood up. She decided that she didn't like how puffy her bra made the top half of her body look so she took the bra off without removing her silk blouse. I told her she looked great, and she complimented me on my hair and asked what I planned to do for the night. The night was open and unplanned, and I told her so. Now that I potentially had another student, and one that would pay more than Yvan, part of me felt that I was moving up in the world. I didn't really know how I felt about it, but I might have to carry myself more professionally and that's what I told Shannon. She laughed and part of me felt sorry for her. She was pretty and intelligent, but she was also one of those people who didn't seem to know what to do with themselves.

"You don't have to worry about me," she said.

"If you say so."

"Oh, you should go to Ladies Night at Lino's."

"Who's Lino?"

"It's not a who. It's a what," said Shannon. "Lino's is this bar outside of town. I'm surprised you haven't been there, but really I'm not since I don't think you like bars. I can't even picture you at a bar, Charlotte. I see you at a dinner party with rich people, eating cheese and drinking wine or something."

"Eating cheese?"

"Yeah, like a fancy French cheese that it's hard to get over here."

"Oh, stop."

"Actually, you can walk to Lino's, but I wouldn't recommend it," said Shannon. I'd get a cab or get someone to drive you. Does Luc have a car?"

"I don't know. I don't think he does, and I wouldn't ask him to drive me if he did."

"Yeah, it might be weird, like you were telling him that you were sexually available or something," and Shannon laughed. "I don't think you want that. And you're going to need a car if you're sticking around here long term, Charlotte. I can't imagine having to walk everywhere, especially now since you're getting busier. And I assume you're still giving lessons to that boy?"

"Yvan's 25," I told Shannon. "Hardly a boy."

"When did he turn 25?"

"His birthday was in October. Soon after I met him."

"Well, he's younger than I am. I'm 35. I know I don't look it, but I am."

"So modest."

"You know what? I can give you a ride to Lino's if you're dead set on going. It's out of the way, but at least you won't have to pay for a cab."

Shannon turned off the radio as she'd had enough of the static. We heard the sound of people arguing through the walls, and we both laughed at the idea that at least it wasn't Shannon arguing with Kurt, her boyfriend. Shannon glanced at her bed and tried to hide all the newspaper articles and letters she had about Rutherford, but I'd already seen them. I wondered what Kurt thought about all that, but I suppose he either didn't care or didn't know the full story. We put on our coats and left Shannon's apartment. Outside, we got into Shannon's car, and she took the interstate even though she didn't have to. She said she just didn't want to take the roads in town because she found them depressing, and once a group of teenagers tried to break into her car when she was stopped at a stoplight. When we reached Lino's outside of town, she put the car in park and turned to me. She said: "You shouldn't think too much about this whole thing I have with Rutherford." I said that she must have known that I would be curious about it when she told me.

"I don't think we should talk about it anymore. Anyway, get out of the car and enjoy your ladies' night."

"I don't think I want to go to ladies' night," I told Shannon. "I'm suddenly feeling respectable and maybe I should go somewhere else and eat cheese."

"Well, being respectable won't get you very far in this life. And no one likes a goody-two-shoes. Go meet a man who can set you ablaze."

"Oh God, what does that mean?" I said and laughed. "You mean light my fire times a hundred?"

"You'll find out!" Shannon shouted giddily at me as I stepped out of the car.

A man in a football jersey smoking a cigarette

was standing by the door, and I walked in. I immediately noted a skew in the ratio of men to women. There were five or six men against two or three dozen women. The women were mostly over 40. And the young men weren't walk-ins off the street. They were shirtless men all dressed the same and carrying trays of drinks. The scene reminded me of the masculine environment of the seminary, only here the men were half naked. I accepted a drink from a man holding a tray, and he told me that the first drink was free, but if I wanted more drinks or food I'd have to pay at the bar. I didn't plan on staying long enough for more drinks, so I thanked him and walked to a corner. From my corner I observed that a young man nearby was being accosted by some rapacious looking women. The women pulled at his bowtie and belt playfully and possessively at various times. He wore a bowtie but nothing else on his tanned torso. There was something alluring and absurd about his get-up, and there was little wonder the women teased him. If we could call it teasing.

There was a seedy quality in the interaction between these women and the boy they'd cornered, but it was difficult to look away. I became less attentive to my surroundings in watching them. My elbow struck the drink table that was behind me, one of those wobbly tables that bars always have for people to set their drinks on. When an empty glass shattered on the floor, I covered the mess with a small napkin.

My attention returned to the other women. There was something false in the way the women interacted with him, and it was clear the victim didn't enjoy it. For that's what he was: their victim. The women were well-dressed, one even wore a chinchilla coat, and the boy was hardly dressed at all, as I've already described. He was younger than they were, probably a local mill-worker by day and hardly in a position to refuse their attentions.

"He's just there to make them happy," a man's deep voice said. "He doesn't care."

I tensed up as I hadn't noticed that anyone had joined me in my corner.

"What did you say?" I asked.

"I said the guy's just there to make the women happy so there's nothing wrong with it, if that's what you were thinking."

"Oh, is that your opinion," and I glanced away from the man and had another sip from my drink.

"Yes, it is," said the young man, who was in the same state of undress as the others. "This isn't really your scene, is it?"

"I don't think that's any of your business. And if you came to peddle another drink, I'm not interested."

"I came to talk to you," said the man.

"Why?"

"Because you're pretty and different from the other women here."

"That's a pretty good line. Good job."

"It's not a line," the man said. "You know you're a knockout and it's only natural for a guy like me to point it out. You know, I like to think I'm a knockout too."

I laughed and said: "Go on."

"What's your name?"

"Charlotte."

"No, your real name."

I laughed again.

"That is my real name," I said. "I know it's old-fashioned, but we don't choose our names."

"I'm only joking. I knew it was your real name. You don't seem like the type to give a fake name. It wouldn't even occur to you. I just wanted you to loosen up a bit."

"Loosen up a bit for what?"

"So we can move around the floor. You know, dance?"

"I'm not a dancer."

"You don't have to be a dancer to dance. And you have a beautiful dancer's body."

"Oh, that's nice," I said. "You're good at this, chatting women up. You're not new at this obviously. And you never told me your name."

"I'm Nate."

"No, I want your real name."

"That is my real name," said Nate. "That's a beautiful perfume you're wearing, Charlotte."

"Thank you, but I'm not wearing any perfume."

"Ah, then it must be a pheromone or something. You know, the kind the black widow spider secretes in order to attract her prey before she eats him?"

Nate put his arm around me. He was very muscular and in this position I felt the warmth of his body.

"No, I think my friend who drove me here probably rubbed some of her perfume on me. That's what your smelling. It's not a pheromone. And you're wearing something too. It's a little too sweet-smelling to be really masculine, but it suits you. One of these vultures rubbed her perfume on you, I guess."

"No, it's cologne," said Nate. "It's mine. It's a little sweet, but some people like that. Some women are intimidated by muscular men, they think we're unapproachable, so a sweet cologne can help break the ice." Nate cleared his throat. "I hope you won't think me rude, but you seem a little out of place here."

"What gave me away?"

"You don't have that air of desperation the other women have. You seem like you're making mental notes of everything for your next book."

"I am a little out of place," I admitted. "This is my first bar trip since I moved here. I've been here a few months now. I work at a diner, but I'm really a teacher."

"A music teacher."

"No, I'm a linguist."

I spoke to Nate for a while and he told me that he'd attended the state college in the neighboring town for two semesters but dropped out because he couldn't balance the social life and school. He'd gotten a job as a personal trainer and was doing very well, or so he said. He'd bought a house, owned two cars, and was able to send money to his younger siblings. I found that last part hard to believe, but he assured me it was true. The more he spoke, the more natural he became. His muscles seemed to relax, which I could discern because he was shirtless. When a bead of sweat collected on his brow, he left if there. He asked me if he could get me a drink from the bar. We were warming to one another, and the other women seemed to be growing envious. I could see them eyeing me from their corner. They'd gotten bored of the man they'd been preying upon.

"No, I don't want anything to drink," I said. "Thanks. And I just realized I don't have a ride home. I'll have to walk back."

"No, I'll drive you. I've done my time. Two hours, but it feels like four. I don't care if Lino doesn't pay me the whole $200. I don't need the money anyway."

I asked Nate why he did ladies nights if he didn't need the money, and he muttered something about getting out and meeting people. He had a magnetic aura and people like him weren't happy when left to their own devices. That was my own conclusion. I got into Nate's car, and he said that he'd like it if we stopped by his place, if I didn't mind. I'd already decided that I wouldn't go home with Nate if he asked.

He said he had an Italian travel book that he could give me. I told him that I didn't speak Italian, that it wasn't one of the languages that I'd studied.

"But it's similar enough to French," said Nate. "You can figure it out. It's a book about a street in Florence."

I didn't believe that Nate actually had the book, but I was curious about what the inside of his house looked like: the house he'd bought with his personal training money. I thought the floors would be littered with free weights or the walls would be plastered with bodybuilding posters, but it wasn't like that at all. Nate's house was ponderous and sedate and had crown molding and wainscotting. It was the sort of house that your best friend's wealthy aunt lived in when you were growing up and which you had the chance to visit once or twice, admiring how the other half lived. Sherry nodded her head in understanding as I related this observation. Nate led me up the central staircase, past the buck heads mounted on the wall and the framed Audubon prints. He led me to a closet where he rummaged through a box and finally unearthed the book he'd told me about. I actually gasped as I hadn't expected there to be any book. It was an oversized book with an excessive amount of detail about a fairly random historic street in the old part of Florence.

In order to reach the book, Nate had to remove several magazines from the box. The magazines were issues of *Men In Fur Coats*, which was a magazine I'd never heard of. I soon learned that Nate had not only appeared in *Men In Fur Coats* multiple times, but had graced the cover twice. He said his favorite fur was mink, but both times he'd been on the cover he'd been dressed in lynx fur. The models didn't choose the fur they wore. He said the heaviness of mink fur really turned him on but that wasn't necessarily a bad thing considering the kind of magazine it was. "But I was never naked though," he said. I told him that it was good that he hadn't been naked in any of his shoots. He never knew what he might want to do with his life when he got older.

Nate laughed and said: "Hold on, let me put on a shirt."

He was still dressed in just his black slacks and bowtie from ladies' night at Lino's. He left the room, and when he returned he wore a red and white flannel that he was buttoning up as he walked in. He was more appealing this way, in this act of dressing himself. His hair was naturally blond and he was athletic, but he still seemed to be molded from the same clay as Paul and Yvan. Nate had an ease and a charm about him, and I think I might have felt less strong about Yvan if I had met Nate first. Nate would have thrown off everything. He had descended the stairs to the kitchen to fetch refreshments, and he returned with two ice waters with limes. The limes were a nice touch, and as Nate handed them to me he suggested that we venture to his bedroom where there was a view out to the creek behind the house. It was the best place in the house to see the creek Nate said. I communicated my disbelief about this creek, and Nate told me that not only did he have a creek, but it was the most pristine creek in town. Nate was unusually good-looking. He was like the man in the TV movie who rescues a woman from drowning or like the most carefully-shaped gingerbread man in the batch.

Nate led me to his bedroom, and the view out onto the creek from the dormer window was forgotten. We sat on the edge of the king-sized bed. He kissed me first on the cheek and then on the lips. He kissed the tops of my breasts, pulling down the top of my blouse in the process. I allowed my hand to fall on his thigh and I imagined that the muscles I felt there were made out of spiced cookie dough. Ginger, nutmeg, cloves and salt are common ingredients in gingerbread dough, but you have to make sure not to add too much salt. The muscles of Nate's legs tensed and relaxed in concert with the muscles of the rest of his body. Nate used a hand to guide my face closer to his. We kissed again, but not for long. I pulled his hand down.

"I can't," I said.

"You can't?"

"No, there's someone else."

"Who?"

"It's someone I'm tutoring at the seminary school. A student."

"You can't kiss me because of your student?" Nate asked.

"Yes. We're close. It won't lead to anything, but it feels like a betrayal. Oh my God. This isn't real."

"It is, Charlotte."

"Sometimes I feel like I'm the only one that's real."

Nate drove me home and was a perfect gentleman about it. As I sat beside him in the car, I imagined him driving back to Ladies Night at Lino's and going home with a different woman. Drunk with desperation, she'd be happy to pretend to see the creek even though it was nighttime and nothing would be visible. She'd wake up in the arms of a personal trainer with 5% bodyfat and muscles that she didn't know the names of. Sartorius. Teres minor. Perhaps Nate would tell her all about Teres minor and how to develop it. But I didn't have long to ponder Nate's misadventures. I put a kettle on because I wanted to have tea even though the caffeine would keep you up at night. Just when I was turning the knob on the stove, I heard the low buzz of the apartment buzzer outside. I pressed the button to open the door, assuming it was Nate and I'd left something in his car. But when I heard the slow, diabolical knock at the door, I knew it wasn't Nate. It was Maxime. I had already changed into my nightgown, but it had a gauzy jacket that I tightened as Maxime walked in.

"You're lucky we're friends," I offered.

"Is that what we are?" Maxime asked.

He sized up my modest apartment and practically scoffed at me.

"What do you want? I shouldn't even have opened the door for you."

"But you did," said Maxime.

He carried a knapsack of aged, European leather. I knew it was an expensive kind of bag because I'd seen rich boys in college with bags like these. With these leather bags, a scratch adds character to the bag rather than defaces it. It's high-quality leather. Like many of the other seminary students, Maxime sprung from a comfortable, traditionalist family. These were the families that liked to have a boy in the priesthood for bragging rights. These men all had a certain generic look to them, like Yvan, even if Yvan was better-looking than they generally were. We sat at the table with chairs that I had against a corner in the living room. The only other place to sit was my bed.

"What's in the bag?" I asked Maxime.

"Wouldn't you like to know. It's a nice view you've got out to the street from here. You can even see into my house."

"Is that what this is about? You think I've been watching you? Why would I?"

"No, the other way around," said Maxime, and he removed a stack of Polaroids from the leather bag. "I've been watching you. Beautiful breasts. Not that large admittedly, and I like 'em big, but they're a pretty shape. Feminine. And they look even better with the bra off."

"Oh my God," I said, perusing a dozen or more photos of me in various stages of undress.

In some of the Polaroids, my face was obscured by the diaphanous, billowing curtains of the apartment, but you could still tell it was me. I could tell and obviously so could Maxime.

"You took these without my knowledge," I told Maxime. "You're gross and it's illegal."

"No, you're gross, if these pictures are anything to go by. Just showing your breasts off to all comers. Anyone seeing these photos would reach that conclusion. I wonder what Yvan would think if he saw them. When he sees them, I mean. I wonder what the dean at the seminary will think. Or what about the parents of that high school boy you'll be tutoring in French soon? A little birdy told me about that. Congratulations, Charlotte."

"What do you want?"

"I want you to do something for me."

"What?"

"You're getting awfully close to Yvan," said Maxime. "That's good. Honestly, I'd like to see you get even closer. I want you to open him up. And I mean really open him up."

"Open him up?"

"Seduce him, Charlotte. And none of this demure, good girl shit. We're talking slutty Catholic school girl, look under my dress and see my bush type shit. The things that Catholic school girls do but don't tell Daddy about. The next time you go to see Yvan, I don't want you to wear any underwear. And I want to make sure he gets a nice look at what you've got going on under there."

"That's disgusting."

"It is, but so are you. Prove me wrong. Tell me why you came to this town, and if it's something perfectly innocent, we'll let the whole matter drop."

"You're horrible. You're a horrible human being."

"Maybe I am."

"When do you want me to do it?"

Maxime laughed, instantly losing the last vestiges of youthful charm he'd had. He'd been sweet before, but now all the sweetness was gone.

"That's what I thought," Maxime said.

"I'm meeting Yvan at the seminary tomorrow," I said. "I can do it then."

"No, no," said Maxime. "That won't work at all. There are two problems with that. First, I don't want the other boys at the seminary to get a look at your bush, just Yvan. And second, I need to see this as it happens so I know that you actually followed through. You'll do it right here in your apartment. When you meet Yvan tomorrow, you tell him that you have something to give him after his lesson. You two can get a cab from the seminary. I'll even give you the money for a cab. I'll be watching from my bedroom window. Do what you gotta do, show him your lady business, whatever. Shake that perky little ass. After Yvan leaves, I'll come by and give you the photos and the negatives."

"Why are you doing this, Maxime? You don't even know me. You don't know anything about me. You don't know what I've been through already. Please don't do this. Just listen. Let me be frank with you."

"Here we go. Book 1 of *War and Peace*. I don't have time for that shit. Maybe some other time, Charlotte. I have to say, it really is a beautiful name. And the woman it belongs to isn't half bad either. At least the parts I've seen so far."

Maxime gathered the Polaroids and walked out of the apartment. He glanced rapidly and furtively at me, and he shut the door softly behind himself.

"It isn't real," I said to myself. "It isn't real. It isn't real. It isn't real."

The kettle suddenly hissed on the stove, as if it had been waiting for Maxime to leave.

"I'm the only one that's real," I told myself.

8

NOVEMBER 15, 2008

I noticed a beautiful woman standing in the courtyard of the apartment building as I returned home from a day's shopping, but I continued on to the apartment where I was dealing with a clogged kitchen sink. The super had told me earlier that he was too busy to help and advised me to purchase a chemical that he said would dissolve any clog. All you needed to do was pour it into the drain and wait a couple hours. When I reached the kitchen, I hitched up my sleeves and unscrewed the cap of the solution. I poured the allotted amount and waited for it to take effect. Later, I returned to the kitchen sink to discover it still clogged. An ominous smell hovered in the apartment. When I called the super, he didn't answer so I locked my apartment door and ventured down to his unit on the first floor. There I found the woman that I'd seen earlier when I was coming home. She was arranging tall potted plants that were like small trees near the super's door. When I knocked on his door, the woman stopped what she was doing to face me. She told me that the super wasn't busy and that he'd only be a moment. She called him Pierre, which was his name, although I'd never heard him called that before. When I finally saw Pierre, he man was holding an old portable television and appeared happier than I'd ever seen him.

"I'm sorry about your clogged drain, Miss," he said. "You probably just need a plunger to bring up whatever's clogged. Sometimes you have to do that after pouring the solution down. I'll be up to join you in a minute."

The woman, Lise, smiled at me and we talked while waiting for Pierre to return with a plunger and whatever else he planned to take up with him to my apartment. She told me that she'd recently moved in, though she'd been dating Paul on and off for many years. "You've probably seen me at the antique store," she said, since she worked at the only decent antique store in town. She was able to use her finds to improve Pierre's apartment as she could purchase items at a discount. Later, she would invite me to the apartment she shared with Pierre and show me her treasures, which included many brass decorative objects and valuable furniture: end tables and chairs. She told me she was throwing out Pierre's imitation leather couches where the fabric stuck to the back of your legs when you were wearing shorts and left black marks. Sometimes the owner of the antique shop took Lise with her when she went traveling to other towns in the state in an old van, and they made a killing because the townsfolk in the bigger towns were willing to pay more for the same items than the locals were.

By the time I was able to join Pierre in my apartment, he had already resolved the issue with the kitchen sink with the plunger.

"I met Lise," I told Pierre. "She's really nice."

"Thank you," said Pierre. "She just moved in. You shouldn't have any more problems with your sink. Call me if anything else clogs."

Afterward, I called Yvan with no answer, so then I went down to the first floor to ask Pierre what to do about a small crack that had appeared in my ceiling. I met Lise again, and she was being so friendly that I told her I could get her a free meal at the diner. In fact, I wasn't sure that I could, but I'd find a way to convince the cook to agree. I'd tell him she was a critic for a local newspaper if I had to. All Lise would have to do is appear with a notepad and a pencil and look official. Since I was just about to go to my shift, I suggested that she come around five, which would be close to when my shift was ending so we could leave together.

Lise arrived and the other workers in the diner

treated her like royalty since I'd lied and told them all sorts of stories about her. She was mostly finished eating when my shift was over, so I joined her in her booth. The window near the booth overlooked a spot outside the diner where the snow was mostly untouched. Lise didn't seem as happy as she'd seemed when I was with her back at the apartment building. She was the sort of person who was happiest when everything around her was bustling and the people were all busy and bouncing off the walls. Lise was pretty because she kept herself up well and dressed to advantage. Her brown eyes were large and expressive, and her small teeth seemed to suit her face. She told me that there had recently been other men in her life besides Pierre and she had only moved in after Pierre convinced her that they should take a more serious route. They might even get married. But Lise didn't think that she was the sort of person that could settle down with one man, especially if it was someone like Pierre. Pierre was the superintendent at a downtown apartment building and not the president of a lumber distribution company, which was the kind of person Lise had been sleeping with before.

Lise asked me about my family, which was more than Yvan or Shannon had ever done. I told her that my mother had left when I was very young, and I had been raised by my father who seemed to take out all his unhappiness about my mother leaving on me. I was an ally in his misery, and I was happy when relatives would come to take me to the beach or to the golf club. Lise seemed to relate although she said that it had been her father that had left. Her father had met a well-travelled saleswoman and had moved to California. The woman was married, and only a week after this woman's husband died, Lise's father died too so he wasn't able to marry her like he wanted. Lise said she liked working in her high-end antique shop because she imagined that all the things inside belonged to her and she was only allowing other people to look at them. This had been easy to do as Lise had been living in an apartment above the shop for several years. Lise had sprung the idea of moving in with Pierre suddenly on her employer and had only been able to keep her job by promising that her hours or work intensity wouldn't change. The owner of the antique shop was possessive and probably was interested in Lise sexually. That's what Lise said though she didn't provide any details.

I walked home with Lise, and my feet were cold from the snow because I hadn't worn weather-appropriate shoes or brought any with me. I'd been in a rush to make it to work and had somehow forgotten the snow like you misplace an item that you always see and should know the whereabouts of. At the apartment, I checked my answering machine where I discovered two messages from Nate, much to my surprise. He said that he had an emergency that he needed me for and asked that I call him immediately. I did, and

shortly afterward I was meeting him in his car outside my apartment building. Nate had a small car big
enough for one or two people, and although I frequently drove with Yvan and Maxime in a car similar
to this, I had a great fear of these kinds of cars as I'd
been in a car accident many years ago that had left
me with a scar on my legs. That's why I generally wore
stockings even though the scar had mostly healed. I'd
been driving with a boyfriend at the time and the car
had crashed in such a way that my leg was pinned
against the chassis of the vehicle. I was in and out of
the hospital for a month and had a long recovery. It
was almost worth it for the devotion that I received
from those around me.

Nate told me that he was having an issue with
his ex-wife. They hadn't been married for long. As we
drove to this woman's house, he explained to me what
had happened. He'd discovered that his ex-wife had
entrusted their daughter to an irresponsible babysitter that would leave the child, Marla, with the babysitter's biological children, who were in their early
teenage years. Nate hadn't known about the babysitter until his ex-wife asked Nate to pick Marla up
from the babysitter's house one day. The babysitter
wasn't home and had left the children alone. The kids
let Nate in and he sat with his daughter and the babysitter's other children until the babysitter returned.
Nate went ballistic about this on the phone with his
ex-wife, he told me, and the ex-wife retaliated by

attempting to get Nate's visitation rights taken away. Nate had gotten a phone call that morning informing him that complaints had been made about him by his ex-wife, and that he had a court date regarding his visitation. Nate explained that he hoped that I could convince his ex-wife to drop the complaints and agree to joint custody.

"I don't see how I can be of any help," I told him. "I just met you, Nate, and to your ex-wife I'd be little more than the other woman. It might make things worse."

"No, it won't," said Nate. "She's only doing this out of spite and it might help to have someone talk to her who isn't me."

"But what do you want me to say?"

"Just tell her that I love Marla and I only want what's best for her. That babysitter was horrible, and it's best for Marla that she spend time with her dad and not someone like that. Since Rachel can only afford someone like that babysitter, then it's best that I step in. Marla could spend time with me and if I need to I can get my own babysitter. And obviously I'd get a better babysitter than this other girl."

"But Rachel will only see that as an opportunity for you to turn her daughter against her," I told Nate. "She's won't agree to it."

"But we have to try."

Rachel lived on the first floor of her apartment building, and when we got there we had to pass addicts idling in front of the building and the people angrily walking down from upstairs who seemed to walk into us intentionally. Rachel's apartment was a handsome two-bedroom, but the laminate floor was coming up from where a dog had scratched at it, and the floor was warped and discolored from something boiling having been spilled on it. Rachel was sitting with a friend watching a talk show on the television in the kitchen, while the children sat in one of the bedrooms eating pieces of cake off dolls' plates. There was a second child because Rachel had a teenage daughter from her first relationship. She was fathered by a man that Rachel hadn't been married to and who had in fact been married to someone else. The child wasn't in school and Nate had told me in the car that the older girl was always to be found idling around the apartment building: either in the apartment she shared with Rachel and Marla or in other apartments. Sometimes this older girl didn't return home for days, which always made Marla cry, or so Nate told me. Marla was too young for school, but as she was approaching four Nate was anxious to get her into a pre-school.

As Nate and I tried to reason with Rachel, several waves of associates of hers came by to talk to her and we were frequently interrupted. The whole situation depressed me, and I was sort of depressed on Nate's behalf, just because he had to deal with all these people. I decided that I'd do whatever I could to help him. Whatever he wanted. As Nate had predicted, Rachel seemed to converse more readily with me than with him. Rachel's glances at Nate when speaking to me about him were nothing short of derisory, and I think she envied him his freedom and his education, even if he hadn't actually completed college. He did have his personal training license and could always go back to school to get his bachelor's. Rachel was a difficult person, but I was able to convince her to drop the complaint that she had against Nate regarding his visitation rights. I agreed with Nate that he should have joint custody, and I told Rachel so, but I thought they could resolve that later. I told Nate in the car that he'd probably have to find an attorney who was skilled at these things. As I drove back to my apartment with Nate, I couldn't help but feel sympathy for Nate, having to deal with concerns that people so young shouldn't have to deal with.

Nate dropped me at the corner of my street, some fifty feet or so from my apartment, and he thanked me as I left the car. As I walked the remainder of the sidewalk to my apartment building, I was surprised to find Yvan's friend Joanna standing on the steps up to the building's front door. She looked different than when I'd seen her at the concert with Yvan and Maxime, but it was still clearly her. Her hair was sedately pinned up today and she was wearing flat shoes. She approached me as I neared her, and I can best describe my stance as guarded.

"You're pretty," she said.

"What does that have to do with anything?"

"You don't have to be rude."

"Well, I don't know what you want. I don't mean to be rude."

"I want to know what your intentions are with Yvan."

"Don't be silly," I said. "Yvan's in seminary school. What intentions could I have?"

"But you're attractive and you seem to like him."

"I could say the same about you."

"Fine," said Joanna. "I like Yvan, but he's studying to be a priest, so I'm backing off and I suggest you do the same. Besides, I have a boyfriend."

"Well, I'm sure your boyfriend would be happy to know that you're obsessed with a man that's not him. A man who's studying to be a priest, like you said."

"We went to college together."

"Fine. I'll be sure to let Yvan know you stopped by and that you were concerned about him."

Joanna shrugged and began to walk away.

"You'll get bored with him," she said. "You'll be intrigued at first because of the whole boxing thing and those hidden scars that he has. There's something exciting about that. And he's studying to be a priest, and that's exciting too. Something forbidden and interesting. We're only human. And Yvan has a certain look to him, but there isn't much besides that. You'll see. And he won't be good-looking forever."

"Why don't you just go away? I'm Yvan's tutor. That's it."

"All right, Charlotte", said Joanna, and she disappeared down the street.

As I entered the building, I saw Lise walking into the apartment that she shared with Pierre. I greeted her, but she didn't say anything to me and shut the door. She was apologetic when I saw her the next day on my way to work, but it was only a week later that she was packing her bags and moving back to her apartment above the antique shop. I imagined her walking through the narrow spaces of the shop, packed with furniture, and explaining to the shop customers where she had gotten this piece or that as if it all belonged to her.

9

NOVEMBER 16, 2008

Nate called me the following day because he wanted me to go with him to visit the Findlaters, who were the couple that owned the gym where he worked. He told me that Tom Findlater ran the gym, but because Tom's wife had paid for the site and for the gym to be built, she was officially the owner. As Nate explained it to me, the Findlaters played an important role in Nate's life because if they decided to open another branch of the gym in a different town, they would likely leave Nate to manage the original gym where he worked. That's what he wanted. As he spoke all I could think of was how he had to time to plan anything with his daughter living in that apartment like she did. Nate said: "You don't have to worry about me, Charlotte. I know how gentle you are. You spend all your time thinking about other people. You can't help it. You're a good person." I told Nate that I'd go to the Findlaters with him, but that I could only stay for two hours at most since I was busy with other things. As I left the apartment with Nate, I ran into Paul Boyer, who was pouring a canister of gas into his car. He didn't see me as I passed him, and I gathered that his car must have died shortly after he arrived downtown. His car wasn't parked properly, and he was standing with another seminarian that I had seen before but whose name I didn't know.

The Findlaters were visibly wealthier than how Nate had described them on the phone, and to reach their door we had to pass through a gate, drive up a driveway, and walk through a pair of stone lions that guarded the steps. Nate knocked on the door and Darcy Findlater was quick to answer. Darcy had a New York accent and we learned that she'd been a high society wedding planner before she'd married Tom. Tom was from this area and had met Darcy while visiting New York for a conference. When Nate and I arrived, Darcy was nearly done preparing dinner and Tom was just about to sit down. There wasn't any-one else coming other than Nate and me. Darcy was a chatterbox and had a way of cutting you off before you finished speaking. She said that she liked my coat and asked me where I had gotten it. But before I was able to answer, she said: "You probably got it at the store next to the hardware shop because I think I saw a coat like that in the window." Darcy and Nate got to talking about the other gym Darcy had mentioned she wanted to open, but it seemed like a poor business decision as the current gym wasn't doing as well as Darcy and Tom would like.

"But a lot of times the problem is you just need more publicity," said Nate. "People will drive for an hour to get to a gym they like, and Findlaters Gym is just that kind of place. What you should do is open a second gym, and that will get your name out there more and drive business to the first gym."

"I agree," said Tom.

"That's easy for you to say," said Darcy. "You're not paying for it," and she took a sip from her wine. "Charlotte, you're not drinking?"

"No, I'm the one that has to drive Nate home," I said. "He's already had two."

"Two's nothing," said Nate. "It's just wine."

"No, let Charlotte be the designated driver," said Darcy. "She's a good girl and we need more of those. I'm surprised no one's taken you off the market yet," like I was a teddy bear at the toy store.

You sure you don't want that pink one, little boy?

"Don't give Nate any ideas," said Tom.

"Oh, it's not like that," I said. "Right?" and I looked at Nate.

"Right."

In my discomfort, I noticed that the Findlaters had a large clear bowl on a stand near the door to the living room, and the thought occurred to me that they were swingers. Nate mentioned that the dinner was delicious and made eye contact with me. The nod of his head he gave me alerted me that he understood my intention to leave, since we'd been with the Find-laters for nearly two hours at the point. As we left, Darcy and Tom asked Nate how his daughter was as they hadn't seen her in some months. At one point, he had brought her to the gym regularly, but they hadn't seen her in some time. Nate was mostly mum on that point but said that he and his daughter were surviving.

In the car, I hit a curb when we exited off the inter-state onto a street that led to the 24-hour convenience store. I glanced at Nate, but all he did was laugh. "I'm clear-headed enough to drive, Charlotte," I thought he'd say, but he didn't say anything. I dropped him at home, and we agreed that I'd park his car on my street tonight and then meet him somewhere the next day to give him back his car. When I got to the apartment building, I parked in the spot where I had seen Paul Boyer before, but I hit the curb again. I hadn't driven a car in two years.

When I got in the car the next morning to return it to Nate, I noticed that the tire that had hit the curb was low on air, and I made a mental note to tell Nate about it. As I entered the car to drive to Lino's where Nate and I had incomprehensibly agreed to meet for breakfast, I caught sight of Yvan walking into Maxime's house. I stopped to watch him, simply standing beside the car with the driver's side door open. Seeing Yvan was like remembering something out of a dream because something had changed between us.

I saw Nate as soon as I walked into Lino's, but I made a performance of pretending not to know where I wanted to sit. Nate was sitting in a booth, and there were two men sitting at the bar by the display of gingerbread people and gumdrop cakes. I journeyed to Nate's booth, where he was intermittently sipping on a heavily-creamed cup of coffee. His head was turned out the window as I sat across from him.

"I like a lot of creamer in my coffee, see," he said when he turned to face me.

He showed me the inside of his coffee cup.

"Is that supposed to mean something?" I asked.

"No, I guess it just means that I actually like the creamer more than I like the coffee."

"I'm sorry I'm late."

"There's nothing to be sorry for. You drove me home," said Nate. "You didn't have to do that."

I told him that one of his tires was low on air.

"Oh, it's fine. I'll put some air in it."

A woman was walking down the street with her child and at one point the child petulantly pulled its hand away from its mother. The child must have been about three or four. "People can be so cruel," I said to Nate. "To me that's cruel." Nate sipped from his coffee, and I noted how bedraggled the neighborhood around

Lino's looked in the daytime. There were addicts and unemployed millworkers hanging about outside. A man had a leather jacket advertising his membership in the lumber shovers union, but I didn't know what a lumber shover was or if there still were lumber shovers. He probably had gotten it at an antique shop. You could see how bare the trees were without leaves or snow. From a window I could see the logging canal that ran behind many of the houses and businesses in this part of town. It was like an idea that held all in the town together.

We both ordered breakfast, and when it came Nate ate avidly. He never looked at me. He had a way of eating very quickly and childishly, which I found endearing. His cheeks were puffed out like a squirrel's with all the food that hadn't been swallowed yet. When we were done eating, Nate suggested we drive back to his house, and I agreed even though I'd already seen it. When we got there, he gave me a tour as if I was a relative who'd come from out of town only to find that Nate was doing better than anyone in the family had reason to expect. He was doing better than anyone realized, even better than he himself knew. We stood at a window of his house and watched the cars drive by. We heard when the drivers were consumed by road rage and honked their horns furiously at one another. We saw how the people in the neighborhood who were walking on the sidewalk would stop and have long conversations with others they came across on the road. We imagined all the inane things they must have said to one another. We couldn't hear them, but we could imagine how inane they must be. As night fell, we watched how the leafless trees took on a melancholic, devoid-of-hope quality. Nate said my hair looked like foxes darting out of their foxholes.

Nate wore his flannels and duck trousers tight-fitted like a workman who didn't want to get any loose material caught in anything. He dressed the part of the logger or millworker even though he wasn't one and didn't want to be one. Perhaps this was how a lumber shover dressed. I was tired of fixating at the things outside of his window, and I walked to the couch. Nate followed and sat beside me.

"Being a personal trainer's the perfect job," Nate said.

"Because you can do whatever you want with your time."

"No. Because everyone's happy when they're training with me. Even the out-of-shape people and the people who are miserable all the time are finally happy. It's the endorphins."

We continued to sit like that on the couch until I said: "I can't stay here, Nate. You should drive me home."

On the way home, we stopped at the sports memorabilia store, which Nate told me rarely has anything worth buying. But this time the sports memorabilia store had something Nate wanted. The sports memorabilia store is across the street from the hard-ware store and the clothing store where Darcy thought I'd gotten my coat from. The sports memorabilia store had a signed Patrice Bergeron jersey, which Nate asked the owner to set aside for him as he didn't have much in the way of cash and the store only accepted cash. He didn't want anyone else to get it. Nate told me that Patrice Bergeron was a native of the town of L'Ancienne-Lorette in Quebec and had played five seasons with the Boston Bruins. After Nate dropped me off at my apartment building, I entered and walked up the stairs, where I found Shannon waiting for me on the third floor. She disappeared behind her ajar door and I followed. I expected to hear the sounds of her fighting Kurt, her boyfriend, but instead I smelled the dinner she'd made wafting out of the apartment and into the hall. Shannon said: "I know you're out there, Charlotte." I entered the apartment and she peaked her head out of the kitchen, finding me in that narrow corridor that linked all the rooms in the larger apartments like hers. She suggested I go into her bedroom.

The room was heavily scented and feminine just like you'd expect. There were flowers everywhere and I suddenly felt sad for Shannon because this felt like the scene in the movie where the person who's about to die is shown in a positive light before they're murdered. The smell of the flowers in the room. The incessant bright blue of the petals. Shannon had a vanity mirror that reached nearly to the ceiling, and the room seemed warm and inviting. She appeared at the doorway soon after I entered. Grabbing a massive stool, she set it beside the chair that she used for the vanity mirror. She was stronger than she looked. "Sit here," she said. She asked me if I liked the shade of lipstick she wore, and I told her that I did. Her hair was up, and with the lipstick the way that she had it, she looked like a drug dealer's girlfriend. Like she was going somewhere to sell suboxone. Then she asked me why I didn't dress up more, and I told her that I didn't like the kind of attention I got when I dressed up.

"What does that mean?" Shannon asked, turning her face away from the mirror and allowing her eyes to rest on me.

"It means that I want to be a wife, not someone's girlfriend."

"Oh," said Shannon. "Not like me, you mean."

"No, that's not what I meant," I said. "You can get married if you want to. And if you don't want to, that's fine."

"That's a very Charlotte answer," said Shannon. "It's like you're not really saying anything and you're keeping your real character concealed. It's funny be-cause I know so little about you. You're like the little dancer in music box who suddenly appears when you open it. She's beautiful and there's music playing, but you don't know where she came from."

Shannon turned to glance out the window, but the

red curtains were pulled shut. All in the room was flooded with the bastard orange light from the sunlight hitting the curtains.

"Power is the only thing worth having in this world," said Shannon. "Power is the only way to protect yourself."

"And hanging out with Kurt and Spider makes you powerful?"

"In a way it does. You wouldn't understand because you don't have a boyfriend. You don't have any man in your life."

"Actually, I met someone at Ladies Night at Lino's."

"But that doesn't count."

"No, it doesn't count."

"It doesn't count because you're holding out for the priest."

"He's not a priest."

"He's a soon-to-be priest," said Shannon. "Kurt's here."

"What?"

"I said, 'Kurt's here.' I just heard him slide the key into the door."

Shannon got up and took one last look in the mirror before walking out of the room. I heard the sound of her and Kurt talking in the apartment hall, and then he walked into the bedroom where I still sat. He was still wearing his work clothes: his flannels, work hat, duck trousers, boots. He didn't work at the mill, which is what I'd thought at first, but as a mechanic at a repair shop outside of town. It occurred to me that Kurt might kill her one day, and I hoped that she'd marry someone else and get away. If Kurt didn't get her, maybe Rutherford Tracy would. Shannon seemed like the kind of woman who expected to die but wasn't sure which man would do it. She was so sweet in her way, but that sweetness didn't mean anything when all was said and done. Sweetness would just attract the wrong people to you. Shannon sat on the edge of the bed as Kurt stood stiffly by the door and greeted me. She smoothed a crease in her skirt and turned to look out the window again, but the blood-red curtains were still closed.

10

NOVEMBER 20, 2008

Yvan wanted to meet at the house near St. Vincent's Hospital where we'd spent those first melancholic moments together. That was the house where the boy had supposedly been depossessed and where Yvan used to go to study and to be alone. There were leaves floating in the canal as I approached, and I could hear the chatter of schoolchildren as they walked from or to school, I didn't know which. It was only 11 in the morning and I wondered why they would have been out of school so early. Rain was coming, and the leaves of the trees turned themselves lustfully upwards to catch the rain that had not yet fallen. I wondered how they'd learned to do that. I needed to go to the grocery store on my way to meet Yvan at the house, and in my bag I carried not only the books we needed for our French lesson but the pancake mix, butter, and brioche bread that I'd bought at the store. I hoped that the groceries wouldn't leak and stain the book.

Yvan was dressed warmly when I met him, but I wasn't. As directed by Maxime, I hadn't worn any underwear. I wore a knee-length skirt of the kind that I would wear to work at the diner, but underneath I wore sheer black stockings with butterfly stitching flying up the leg. I was four feet away from Yvan on the mattress where we both sat: the mattress that the boy had been tied to while the spirits had been cast out. Maxime didn't want me to do anything while I was alone here with Yvan, so I kept my legs demurely crossed.

"You're cold," Yvan said.

"I'm not," I told him. "I don't feel the cold."

Yvan and I did very little in the way of studying it seemed. He spoke about all the things that were occupying his mind, all the minor things happening at the seminary, and he even told me a little about his family, which was strange as he had seldom brought them up before. Yvan spoke about Paul Boyer, who Yvan seemed to both like and dislike at the same time. I thought there was a part of Yvan that wanted to give Paul a hard jab in the mouth, and this side of Yvan didn't bother me then. I only saw the good things. And Paul could be insufferable at times. Perhaps he didn't deserve a punch to the mouth, but a good shot to the gut wouldn't hurt. Yvan and I didn't stay long at the house and we actually ran into Paul as we were leaving. Yvan had parked his car at the St. Vincent's lot, and for some reason Paul was in the area. He told us that he was volunteering at a Catholic outreach center, but who knew what he was really doing there. Paul waved at us from the parking lot when he saw us. He was looking more heavy-set than when I'd seen him last, which seemed like months. He was tall and squat: a squat version of the square-faced men that worked at the mill, worked in the hardware store, worked in all the other stores and shops, and frequented the bars. You could say Paul was a taller, heavy-set version of Yvan. Paul told Yvan that he should be studying for the theology exam they had that week, and Yvan said that he would after he wrapped up his French lesson with me. Paul laughed at this, but it was a phony kind of laughter, like he was just being polite. Perhaps he wanted to study theology with Yvan. Paul asked Yvan if he'd heard that one of their friends was getting ex-pelled from the seminary for inviting a woman over. Yvan haven't heard, and he turned completely around to face Paul.

"That's not true," Yvan said. "Where'd you hear that?"

"It is true, it just happened today," said Paul. "James Berg is getting expelled because he had a woman over yesterday after he'd already been caught doing that before. They'd told him then that it better be the last time."

Paul sat down beside Yvan on the railing that surrounded the St. Vincent lot.

"Maxime will love that," said Yvan.

"Why would Maxime love that?" Paul asked.

"Because Maxime has a thing for schadenfreude, if you haven't noticed," said Yvan. "All the same, the school wouldn't be the same without him."

"You think that the school wouldn't be the same without Maxime?" asked Paul, incredulous.

"I do," said Yvan.

"Because the rest of us all are all lifeless drones and the only thing that matters in life is being interesting."

"Right."

"Maxime said he wants to meet you later," said Paul. "You should call him or stop by his apartment."

"Why would he tell you that he wanted to meet me? Why wouldn't he just call me?"

"Because I saw him at breakfast and he must have forgotten to call you."

"We could always study some other time," I said softly to Yvan.

"No," said Yvan. "We'll study today. We'll just have to go somewhere else."

Paul disappeared to class, and I walked with Yvan to his car for the drive to my apartment. We were of a like mind that was where we should go, and we approached the car silently, though I was mum for a different reason. Before we reached Yvan's car, we saw the tall, portly figure of a robed man walking towards us. "That's the dean," Yvan whispered to me. Yvan stood apart from me, as if suddenly remembering what he was in seminary school for. He hunched over his bag, checking that he'd brought all his books with him.

"I think you're Ms. Langlois," said the smiling dean.

I told him that I was, and he patted my hand and looped his arm into mine unexpectedly.

"Come walk with me a moment," he said.

We walked back toward the house where I'd sat with Yvan. Yvan remained a few feet away at the car.

"I heard you work at the diner," the dean said.

"I did, but I'm down to three shifts a week."

"Oh, that's too bad," said the dean.

"See ya," said a high school girl to her friend nearby to us.

"And your lessons with Yvan are going well I think," the dean said. "That's what I've heard at least."

I told him that they were, thank you, and he said that I was doing so well with Yvan that I might take on other students. Considering what was soon to pass between me and Yvan, I could not help but laugh at that, though I tried my best to maintain a modicum of respectful composure. It wasn't easy. But the dean mistook my laughter for friendliness, and he continued on in ever more glowing terms.

He said: "I was concerned about Yvan taking lessons from a young woman. Of course, I hadn't seen you before today, but word was getting around about you: that you were the polar opposite of our seminary priests. They were right. You're very young, but you're very good. Yvan is making progress. In fact, he'll be speaking like a native in no time. Of course, the French of our congregation is the Swiss variety, but Standard French is acceptable for now, and Yvan can improve his dialect before he goes to the mother monastery in Switzerland."

"Will he go to Switzerland?" I asked, genuinely surprised.

"We expect that he shall," said the dean. "And you do have your degree in French, don't you, Miss?"

"A master's, yes."

"Well, we might even consider you becoming a teacher here. Wouldn't that be nice?"

Yvan drove me in his Ford to my street, parking right in front of the building. We took the stairs, and I'll never forget the clack my shoes made as we scaled them. Yvan was walking slowly behind me, and even he seemed to think that something momentous loomed above. When we reached my floor, we immediately heard Shannon arguing with Kurt. As we neared my apartment, Shannon's door flew open and Kurt came charging out. He wasn't fully dressed, and as soon as he saw me and Yvan, he said: "Oh, there she is. Maybe she'll mind her own business this time." I told Yvan to ignore them.

"What's his problem?" Yvan asked.

"I don't know. I wouldn't take anything he says seriously," I said.

We walked into my apartment, and after Yvan came in, I closed and locked the door behind me.

"He lives across from you?" Yvan asked.

"No, that's Shannon's boyfriend. Shannon's my neighbor."

We walked to the table in the living room, and Yvan began to remove his books from his bag. It seemed strange to me that he'd so readily agreed to come here to study. I was expecting more resistance, and I began to form the impression that events were unfolding in a fashion that was unavoidable. Part of me hoped that I wouldn't have to go through with it. I was sitting in a chair at the table, but I moved the chair back somewhat so that Yvan would be able to see under my skirt. It was also important that Maxime would be able to see what I was doing from the window. Yvan, who had opened one of his books, gave me a curious look but didn't say anything.

Finally, he said: "It's funny that you want me to translate this poem into English from French, since it was originally in English. *The Rape of Lucrece.*"

"It's a long poem," I remarked. "You didn't read it in high school?"

"No," Yvan admitted. "We read *Hamlet* and *Macbeth*, but I don't remember this."

"Well, we'll see if you get anywhere near to the original."

"That's not fair. It's actually impossible."

Yvan's laugh was restrained, and I moved a hand slowly down my thigh. My legs were crossed. Yvan quickly glanced at what I was doing with my hand and then looked away. He cleared his throat softly and consulted his pocket dictionary for the translation of a word in the text. I uncrossed and recrossed my legs, and suddenly Yvan's attention was fixedly drawn to them. He couldn't pull his gaze away. He held his book firmly in his hand, more firmly than was natural.

"You're squeezing the life out of your book," I noted.

"What?" asked Yvan.

"I said your squeezing the life out of your book."

"No, I'm not. I don't know what you mean."

"That's enough," I said.

I got up and walked to the window, closing the blinds. It was that diaphanous material so it didn't make much difference, but I closed them anyway. In fact, the blinds had been partially closed when Maxime had managed to obtain those pictures of me.

Maxime showed up at my apartment before my 10 o'clock shift at the diner. I don't know how he knew my work schedule, but he knew. I suppose he was always watching me. After I opened the door, he walked into the apartment as if it was his rather than mine. In a way, the space had become as much Maxime's as mine after what had happened, all those times I thought I'd been alone and he'd been watching me.

The idea of him seemed to inhabit the place as much as I did.

"It's a nice place you have here," Maxime said. "I never noticed it before."

"It isn't a nice place. What do you want?"

"Can't I give you a compliment?"

"I don't want any compliments from you."

Maxime walked into my bedroom. I followed him in a fury and watched as he sat on the bed.

"What are you doing?" I asked.

"What does it look like I'm doing," Maxime replied, but he wasn't looking at me.

He smugly sized up the room and I suddenly felt cheap.

"I'm not done with you," he said. "I saw you from the window, and I can confirm you did what you were supposed to. Good girl. But we're not done. I've got one more thing I want from you."

I slowly turned my back to him and began unbuttoning my blouse. When I was only in my bra, I placed the folded blouse gently on a corner of the bed.

"No, no, I'm not interested. You're not my type."

That hurt, but I kept my anger to myself.

"One thing, Charlotte," said Maxime. "Whatever happens, I don't want you to lose your sweetness. That's what attracted Yvan to you in the first place. If you become cheap and angry and used-up, Yvan won't be attracted to you anymore."

I asked Maxime what he wanted, to get to the point,

and he told me that I wasn't done with Yvan. All I'd done was give him blue balls, and we needed to go all the way. Yvan was virile and randy, or so Maxime assumed, and I was a slut, so we had to do what virile young studs and sluts do with one another. 2 + 2 = 4, as far as Maxime was concerned.

"You want me to sleep with him," I said.

"Bingo," said Maxime.

"Why do you care if I sleep with him or not?"

"That's my business. You just need to do what you're told. And I think this time bringing him back to the apartment won't be enough. If I know him, Yvan's already starting to think something's off. I'll have to find another place for you guys to go at it. I have a place in the country, so maybe we'll go there."

"You're too young to have a place in the country," I said, turning away from Maxime.

"I inherited it. It's a cabin and it's the perfect place for two young lovers."

"You're a horrible person," I said. "Aren't you satisfied with what you've done already? How do I know you weren't taking pictures through the window like last time?"

"You don't know."

"What did you say?"

Maxime sighed.

"I'm not taking any more pictures," said Maxime. "You did your job well and I got what I needed."

"And what is it that you need, Maxime? Why are you doing this?"

"Because you deserve it," Maxime said. "You're hiding something. You have the look of someone who's hiding something. No one's falling for this innocent girl shit. Not me, at least. What kind of woman just shows up out of the blue and starts working at the diner, traipsing around in a pearly white pinafore like a character out of a TV show? Something about you isn't right. Why did you come to this town anyway? You know what, I don't care."

"If you can have secrets, so can I."

"Anyway, you like it."

"I like what?"

"The seduction. Seducing a big, strapping boy like Yvan. Wrapping him around your little finger."

"I don't like it. It's demeaning."

Maxime laughed and stood up. His bootheels clacked loudly as he marched out of the room. He was still saying mean-spirited things to me as he walked out. He said that I wasn't done being dragged through the mud so I'd better get used to it. At least I'd better if I didn't want the pictures getting out. And I didn't want the pictures getting out, that was true. At that point in the story, I looked at Sherry who wasn't smiling anymore. She had lit a cigarette, which she smoked, but then she put the cigarette down in an ash tray and stood up. She closed the blinds of her mobile home windows, but not before taking a long look outside first.

11

NOVEMBER 22, 2008

As I took my shower the next morning, I closed my eyes and wondered if I might find myself someplace else when I opened them. Shortly after the shower I received a phone call from Bernard Prevost, who explained that he was Yvan's brother. I'd never met him before, though Yvan had mentioned him in passing. Bernard admitted that Yvan had given him my phone number, and after he said it he laughed politely to break the silence. I could already discern the ways in which Bernard was different from Yvan. Bernard asked me to meet him at Yvan's father's house, where Bernard was staying at the time. He gave me the address and warned me that the house sat some ways outside of town. Actually, it lay between the two old mill towns but a bit closer to the town where I currently lived. It occurred to me to explain to Sherry the locale of the house, but it seemed she already knew. I thought that Yvan must have written her or called her while he was at the seminary. She knew all about Bernard it seemed.

I thought I'd walk to the Prevost house but only because I'd miscalculated the distance. It ended up being much farther from my apartment building than I thought. But I enjoyed walking everywhere, and as I left the town, I heard the thud of the millworkers boots as they trudged to their eating places on their lunch break. I heard them chattering and fighting with one another as working men do. I hadn't been walking long when I realized that it was much too far to walk, and I knew Shannon was on a shift so I couldn't call her. I was standing by a chain restaurant off the inter-state, and from there I could see the forest that was sparser than it must have been when the mill owners moved in. The mill owners had brought the French-Canadian workers, people like Yvan's family. But there were still oak trees with boughs broad enough to cast long shadows over the macadam and the asphalt of the interstate. At times I thought the oak trees might grow legs and walk away from this corner of hell where everything was sweet. I called a taxi since Shannon was busy, and it took almost an hour for the driver to show. I paid the driver what he asked plus the recom-mended tip even though I wasn't happy. I wasn't happy that he was late and that the tip had automatically been set to 20%, but I smiled as I paid it. He'd told me he'd be there within fifteen minutes, and I'd had to stand out in the cold as the people dining in the chain restaurant happily came in and out through the door. When they opened the door, the warmth from inside suddenly rushed out, but then it was cold again when they left. The walls of the restaurant looked like the logs of a log cabin, but when I tapped them I realized they were just imitation wood. One time, a man that was coming out of the restaurant looked me up and down and said to his girlfriend: "What's she standing outside like that for?"

When I reached the Prevost house, I was surprised to see how large it was. It huge if a bit outdated. It sat on a hill above the street and its façade was a mélange of exposed wood and brick like a Tudor-style house in Connecticut. One of Yvan's friends was leaving and he opened the door for me. Inside, the house's walls were paneled in dark woods and hung with masculine paintings: racehorses, jockeys, military scenes. The ceilings were low as they sometimes are in old houses, and the house's halls were narrow like in a shotgun house in town. My eyes were constantly drawn to the staircase, which dramatically dove into the darkened upstairs where it seemed to disappear completely. The upstairs was like a whore's mouth that sucked all the sweet things into it: the rare waft of fresh air from the holidays when the mill was closed or the sweetness of the men who were walking out on the street. I walked into the dining room where an old woman was sitting.

She said not a word the entire night. Yvan explained to me later that she belonged to a tribe of mutes. It was a joke.

Yvan's parents weren't at home. "I see you've met Aunt Marie," Yvan said when he appeared. From the waist up, he was dressed for a night out though I hadn't heard we were going anywhere. He was freshly shaven and wearing a necktie. He told another friend of his who was leaving not to feed the ducks outside: the two duck statues that sat at the foot of the mound of the house, close to the sidewalk. Aunt Marie was eating a salad and drinking a water that smelled like it had been flavored with straight-from-the-beehive honey. The scent of honey circulated in the room. Yvan was wearing worn khaki shorts that I hadn't seen him in before. I'd mostly seen him at the seminary. It was the first time I was seeing him at home. I told Yvan that I hadn't precisely met Aunt Marie and he said: "Aunt Marie, Charlotte. Charlotte, Aunt Marie."

"How are you?" I asked, extending to the woman a hand that she ignored. She looked at me quizzically for a moment and then looked away.

"How was your cab ride?" Yvan asked.

"How do you know I took a cab?" I asked.

"Because it's too far to walk."

"I tried," I said. "But it was too far, like you said."

Yvan smiled and looked down at his hands. I realized then that he cared what I thought about him and didn't know how much of himself to reveal.

"We're not snobs here," he said.

"Aren't you?"

"No. How can we be? Do you like fish?"

"Not really."

"Well, that's too bad as we're having fish tonight. My father told me it's Aunt Marie's favorite dish, but I don't know for sure. Is it true that you wrote a book a few years ago?"

I didn't answer right away, but then I said: "Yes, it's true."

"You don't look like your picture on the book flap," said Yvan. "You were wearing your hair up in it and looking really official. Bernard found the book. I didn't tell him anything. Not even what happened the other day."

"Nothing really happened."

"Well, it felt like something happened."

"I'm glad you didn't say anything."

"Bernard came across the book and found out you lived in town," Yvan continued. "He doesn't live here. He managed to get your book shipped to his apartment and he brought it to the house. I didn't read it, but he did. And don't say you didn't realize people around here read books. They don't read books, but Bernard's different."

"I won't say it then."

"I was surprised when I read that you were from this part of the country. You never talk about that."

"My father and I moved around a lot. He remarried. I think I told you."

"So, he's alive."

"Of course, he's alive."

"I think your father must be like you," said Yvan. "Quiet with a classic kind of face. Features I mean. Just like carefully-formed."

"I don't know what that means, Yvan."

"You never mention your family, and I was starting to think you were made in a factory."

"Maybe I was. Maybe my father is just the scientist who made me."

"Is he?"

"No," I replied. "You're one to talk. You're a factory-made person if there ever was one."

"No, I was made in the mill. My grandfather..."

That was when Bernard walked in, and Sherry couldn't hide her amusement at this point of the story though I hadn't said anything about him yet. He wore a long puce housecoat and his hair was pulled into a long, slick ponytail. His hair was longer and blonder than Yvan's: dark blond and agile like a horsetail. His face was thin, but angular and masculine like Yvan's. Bernard had a singularly attractive quality, and as he walked in the meadowlarks landed on the sill of the window that looked out onto the driveway. Bernard took his seat at the foot of the table, across from Yvan who sat at the head.

"Do I look like how I sound on the phone?" Bernard asked me.

"Yeah, you do," I replied.

"What do I look like?"

"Like someone's who's seen the world."

"Like someone who's seen the world?" Yvan asked, waiting anxiously for dinner to be brought out. "What does that mean?"

"The look of someone who's been somewhere other than this fucking mill town," said Bernard.

"Well, he has," said Yvan. "He went to school in Boston."

"Really?" I asked.

"It's not that surprising," Bernard said. "Even people from around here manage to escape sometimes."

Then Bernard smiled, revealing a row of small front teeth.

"Yvan didn't even tell me that you were here," said Bernard. "That you were giving him lessons I mean. I had to find out about you. I hope he's paying you well."

"I'm not," said Yvan. "Not well at least."

"You don't want anyone to know anything about you," said Bernard, looking at me with sincerity. "Right? You just want to appear one day and then another day, you'll be gone. Like that movie where you realize at the end that the female lead got her name off a headstone in the graveyard and you have no idea who she really is."

Yvan said he had no idea what Bernard was talking about, and then when Yvan tried to change the subject, Bernard said: "Maybe it's none of our business."

"Bernard, shut up," said Yvan. "I was just about to ask Ms. Langlois the series of forty-four questions I prepared."

"Right, Langlois," said Bernard. "You're one of us then. You come from French-speaking people. From this part of the country. Your bio on the book cover didn't go into that," and then Bernard tossed Yvan a help-me-please look.

"Her father's from this area," said Yvan. "Look, I don't know much more than you do. And like you said, it's probably none of our business. I think I know less than you do since you've read her book and I haven't."

Yvan grinned at me and then produced a crumpled piece of paper from a shirt pocket. "All right, so here are my questions that I prepared."

He read the first question.

"Are you that lady that wrote the book that Bernard found? Oh, I already asked that one. Anyway, the rest are stupid so I won't even read them."

"Are you married?" asked Bernard.

"No," I answered.

"Have you ever been married?" was Bernard's next question.

"Not that I can recall."

"You'd probably remember," said Bernard.

"Bernard, she's too young to be married," said Yvan. "And your questions are rude."

"Are they?" Bernard asked. "I'm sorry if they are."

"I don't think they're rude," I said.

"You look like a young Lara Flynn Boyle," Bernard remarked. "Are you related?"

"No."

"Do you want to watch *Welcome to the Dollhouse* on DVD later?"

"Sure."

Bernard spoke with his elbows resting on the table and his body hunched forward a little. This posture revealed both his flat, bony chest and his clavicles.

"You're staring," said Bernard.

Yvan sighed.

"You'll have to excuse my brother," Yvan said. "He only had one manner and he lost that a long time ago."

"You're one to talk," said Bernard.

"You invited this beautiful young woman here because you wanted to ask her if she was married?" Yvan asked.

"No, I invited this beautiful young woman here because everyone's talking about her," said Bernard.

"Are they?" asked Yvan.

"No, not everyone," said Bernard. "I was talking to the dean of the seminary school on the phone and he mentioned that he had met you, Charlotte."

"The dean called?" asked Yvan.

"Yeah, but it was nothing to do with you. He wanted to talk to Dad. I think he wants more money, another donation for the school." And Bernard turned to me. "Did my brother tell you he was engaged before? Her name was Eve and she was even worse than that woman from that movie."

"Which movie?" Yvan asked.

"*All About Eve*. You've never seen it. He doesn't watch black and white movies. Do you watch black and white movies, Charlotte?"

"Sometimes."

"Well, that's an elusive answer," said Bernard. "What do you think about gingerbread men?"

"I don't have an opinion about them."

"You're not getting anything out of her," said Yvan. "I've been trying for months."

"That's not true," I said, perhaps loosening up a little. "I told you about some of my travels when I was younger."

"Yeah, but that's hardly anything."

"Aunt Marie was looking forward to going to Yvan's wedding, but then he decided to go to seminary school instead," said Bernard.

"I didn't decide to go to seminary school instead," said Yvan. "I was made to go. The seminary school wouldn't take you so I had to go."

Then Yvan turned to me.

"We have this thing in the family where one of the sons is supposed to become a priest," he said.

I nodded and Yvan continued.

"It's a good thing too because now Bernard has to be the one to marry Eve. It's gonna be really hard for him as you can probably imagine, even though you just met him. And when you do schedule the wedding, Bernard, you'll have to make sure you don't schedule it on the same day as Aunt Marie's vocal cord surgery."

"Aunt Marie's vocal cord..." Bernard began, entirely duped.

"It's a joke, Bernard. Even Charlotte knew it was a joke. See, she's laughing. There's no surgery in Aunt Marie's future, is there?" and Yvan patted his relative on the hand. "And imagine what she'd say if she could talk. She might turn us all over to the police. For one thing, she wouldn't be happy with the color of that housecoat of yours. What did you call it? Time of the month?"

"Puce."

"That's right. Puce."

"You know, Charlotte," said Bernard. "Laughing like that is the worst thing you can do. All it does is encourage him and he gets too much of that being the golden boy. He doesn't need encouragement. You'll see when you've known him a while. He's no different than those guys you see marching home from work, only his father has a little bit of money from playing hockey."

"Our father," said Yvan. "Our father married the daughter of the president of a lumber company," Yvan went on, turning to me. There was a solemn quality that Yvan's voice took on, and even Aunt Marie craned her head towards him and listened. She rattled her wrist of bracelets and hiked up her shirt sleeves.

"Our grandfather worked at a mill his whole life. Everyone thought Dad would work at the mill too, but then he met a girl and he married her. Then everything changed because the girl's father owned the mill. We don't really have that much money, our family I mean. We have an inheritance from my mother, who's dead, and my father sits on a board or something. We're just common people who stumbled into a little bit of money. This is just a working-class person's house with some flare. In 20 years, it'll be a ruin."

"He calls this being on his best behavior," Bernard said.

"Tell her about the book you're reading now, Bernard," said Yvan.

Under the old coffers of the ceiling and in this seated posture, Yvan looked small.

"It's about how they recruit men for the French Foreign Legion, if you can believe that," Yvan told me. "I think he wants to join."

"I never said I wanted to join," Bernard exclaimed.

"He thinks the first step is that all the guys present their rear ends for an unusually deep prostate exam."

"Oh, you think that's funny?" Bernard asked. "You might be surprised to learn that Yvan read that Foreign Legion book too, Charlotte. I don't mean surprised that he read a book on the Foreign Legion, but that he can read at all."

"It is a little surprising."

"But you taught me my A-B-Ds last year, Bernard," Yvan said. "Remember?"

Bernard turned to me and looked me over more closely than he had before.

"Your father is some kind of skilled professional," said Bernard. "Not a doctor but something like that."

"He's an engineer."

"That's enough with the personal questions, Bernard," said Yvan. "She's a guest."

"Fine, well, we can talk about ourselves then," said Bernard. "We're all incestuous here. I don't just mean this family, but the people in this town. We're all second or third-generation working class people, even if we're not so working class anymore, and we've all intermarried with each other. That's why we all have the same shade of hair and the same head shape. There's a friend of ours named Denis and he's a dead ringer for Yvan. He could be his twin. We're all clones of one another. Incestuous, like I said. Our family is old and the blood is thin and there's only two young men left. You have that dense gentleman at the head of the table, Yvan, ready to eat his dinner with the back ends of his knives like a barbarian, and me, a man who wears fancy housecoats like the good old family fairy."

"If you mean that your family has become degraded, I don't see it," I told Bernard.

"Really?" said Bernard.

"No. Man always believes himself in decline because the Western concept is that Man strives toward some hypothetical state of perfection. In reality, Man is what he is."

"I like that answer," said Bernard. "You may stay and finish your dinner."

"Thank you."

"But don't we all pretend?" Yvan asked, glancing at me suddenly.

"I don't," said Bernard.

"Do you mind if I ask where your father is?" I asked Yvan.

"Hell if I know," said Yvan. "On a business trip?"

Then Bernard said: "I'm actually the elder brother, if you can believe that."

"Are you?" I asked.

"I am."

In Yvan's bedroom, he said: "I'm looking for my boxing gloves." Boxing was something he'd done in college and that he'd wanted to do long before. He had a hard time meeting people or he didn't like the guys he met so he boxed. People who boxed could make friends with their coaches, their sparring partners or even their former opponents. Mr. Prevost was a competitive person and had instilled the same spirit in his boys. Yvan rummaged through the drawers of his bedroom and asked that I look through the closet. I came across many personal things of his in there: his clothes with his smell, schoolbooks that had been bought but never read and were still in plastic, an Easy Bake oven that must have belonged to Bernard. Yvan had hidden it and had forgotten all about it. Although Yvan lived at the seminary, his worn clothes littered the floor of his closet and his bedroom.

"Did you find the gloves?" he asked. "They have to be in there somewhere."

I told him that they weren't. In a drawer I found pictures of Yvan during his boxing days, including one where he was down on his knees in the ring like he'd been knocked out by his opponent. Behind him were the stunned faces in the crowd, as defeated as he was. It was posed. All the pictures were posed because Yvan had never experienced defeat in anything before. He was the man the sperm banks put ads in the newspapers to try to attract, and when he became a priest the number of parishioners attending mass would double because everyone in America likes winners. Only Yvan would never become a priest. I knew that then. But Yvan was a born winner or at least had the look of one.

"Did you find them?" Yvan asked again.

Yvan's words were slurred because he'd drunk too much at dinner.

"Yvan, we need to talk," I said, turning round to face him.

"I already know what you have to say," said Yvan.

"No, you don't. You don't know anything."

"Oh, I don't know anything, do I? You'd be surprised what I know."

I sighed and said: "Yvan, All I've ever done is try to help you."

"Help yourself, you mean."

"Okay. Where is this coming from?"

"I'm paying you, right? You're not working for free."

"Oh, now you want to start being mean."

"I'm not being mean. I'm just telling it like it is."

"So you're an angry drunk. You learn something new everyday."

I walked over to Yvan's bed and sat on a corner of it. I rubbed a spot in my shoulder where the bra strap dug into my skin and I tapped my foot on the floor. "Everything's so easy for you," I said. "You're not real. You're not a real person." Yvan gave up on the boxing gloves and sat beside me. He asked me if I needed to be anywhere tomorrow and if I wanted to spend the night in the house. I told him I didn't have anywhere to be, but I wouldn't stay as it wouldn't be right. Everything reached the dean of the seminary, and what was Yvan thinking anyway? He said he just wanted to lie in the bed with me a while if I wouldn't stay, and I told him we could. He pulled off my shoes slowly and deliberately, an act of gentleness which surprised me. The shoes were uncomfortable in general, and they'd become especially so after walking in them most of the day. We lay beside one another but really far apart. But then Yvan pulled me closer. He put his arm about my waist and I allowed it.

"I lied," he said. "I read your book. Not all of it, but the first few chapters. It's about a woman who falls in love with a seminary student."

"Lots of women fall in love with seminary students."

"No, they don't. It's very specific. And he was a boxer too."

"It's just a story. That's it."

"So that's all this is," said Yvan. "This is just a fantasy that you planned out. You have it all planned out."

Yvan fell asleep with me lying beside him and his clothes strewn everywhere. Yvan slept soundly and quietly like a child, and I didn't want to wake him by getting out of the bed or banging my shoes on the floor as I stepped into them. I managed to step out of the bed softly, and I picked up my shoes. I'd put them on in the hall. I saw the red leather of his boxing gloves in a cracked drawer of the end table on my side of the bed: just a hint of red through a tiny crack. The gloves were squished behind a stack of boxing maga-zines with dog-eared pages. The magazine pages were crumpled as if the men on the covers had sweat right onto them. Grabbing onto the gloves, I used a hand to wipe away the thick dust. Then I sat the gloves on the edge of the bed. Yvan would find them when he woke up the next morning. I considered tidying Yvan's room before I left, but I decided not to. He'd have to manage on his own. As I'd already told him, I wouldn't stay the night.

12

NOVEMBER 23, 2008

"I didn't realize you wrote a book about a woman who falls in love with a seminary student," Sherry tells me, pulling a corner of the curtain in the trailer up to look out the window and interrupting me in my narration. From here we can see the fog-covered field outside and the satellite dish bolted to the side of the hotel.

"It didn't mean anything," I tell Sherry. "That was just something I did before I met Yvan," I tell her.

Sherry takes the kettle off the stove and pours the hot water into two cups where tea bags have already been placed. I told her that I went home from the Prevost mansion after that. I was afraid of running into Maxime there, and I didn't think I could handle Yvan, Maxime, and Bernard all at once. There wasn't any reason why I should be worried about Maxime turning up, but he seemed to occupy my thoughts more than he ever had before. At home, I went to sleep even though it was only midday. I turned off all the lights and covered the windows with sheets since the curtains couldn't keep the lights out. The only way to keep all the light out of the apartment was to take dark-colored sheets and use safety pins to pin them over the windows. I had a terrible dream. In my dream I was sleeping in a doll's house: I was small enough to sleep and live inside of it. A monster scaled the dollhouse to reach me inside. When he reached my bedroom, the monster showed me that he carried a bouquet of lilies, but I didn't care. I woke up screaming.

Though I'd only just left him, Yvan returned to me later in the day. He was more sedate than usual, telling me that he'd gotten a call from Maxime and that we were to go to his cabin.

"I don't want to go to Maxime's cabin," I said.

"But it would be rude not to."

"I don't care. What did he say to you?"

"He didn't say anything. He just wanted us to come over."

"He must have said something, Yvan."

"He said that he was at his cabin in the woods and he wanted us to come over. I think he just doesn't want to be alone."

"That's not what this is about."

"You don't know what this is about, Charlotte," said Yvan. "Neither do I."

Maxime's cabin was larger than Yvan's family house. As Yvan and I drove up in Yvan's Ford, we made out two people in the kitchen. One was a woman engaged in preparing food and the other was a haggard looking man. We met them soon enough. They were the cook and her cousin who served as the groundskeeper on the property. The woman, who had never met Yvan before, looked him over thoroughly and then told us that Maxime was out back.

"I can take you to a room upstairs if you want to freshen up," the woman said.

"We don't need to freshen up," said Yvan. "We're just here for the afternoon."

"All right, but you can go upstairs if you need to use the facilities or take a shower, only don't go to the third floor. That belongs to the staff."

"We got it," said Yvan.

We walked the main wood-paneled hall of the house because Yvan thought there'd be a back door. There wasn't. But there was a bay window at the end of the main hall, and from there we were able to watch Maxime. He was out back using an ax to chop wood. Only he wasn't really trying to chop the wood. He was just trying to look busy. When he decided he was done with the ax, he kicked tennis balls into the back woods behind the house like a vagrant. "I don't know why we came here," I told Yvan. Yvan told me to cheer up, and he used one of his hands to pull my face close to his. It was like we'd already decided to be destroyed together, only we never said anything to one another about it. That's what this sudden closeness was: a decision to be mutually destroyed. Yvan said that we should wait for Maxime to come back into the house. Maybe we should go upstairs and freshen up after all. We chose a bedroom that we were sure no one lived in. The door was ajar, and inside the room was devoid of the personal touches of human occupation. I sat on the seat inside the dormer window and watched as Yvan walked to a sink to wash his face. The bedroom had a sink and faucet right in the room like in an old dorm room or a bed and breakfast. Yvan used a towel to dry off and then he looked at me. He looked like the kind of person whose face you'd see in the newspaper attached to a particular story and say: "That person's handsome." From a distance, he didn't have any obvious scars from boxing other than a mild case of cauliflower ear. But cauliflower ears don't really come from boxing, as Yvan had told me earlier. That must have been the result of an illegal maneuver from a boxing opponent.

Tired of waiting for Maxime, we returned to the ground floor where we found that Maxime had already come in and was sitting with the cook and the groundskeeper in the kitchen. He was drinking Maxwell House and looking suspiciously at us as we entered the kitchen. But when we got closer, Maxime smiled. "There you are," he said. He walked up and patted Yvan on the shoulder. The cook checked the state of the beef she was cooking in the oven, and when she was done she wiped her hands on her white pinafore. She'd already taken off her oven mitts and placed them on the quartz countertop. The look she allowed to fall on Maxime reflected her obeisance.

"Did you guys have a hard time getting here?" Maxime asked.

He was dressed in a relaxed fashion, like when a rich person wants to appear at ease: wearing jeans and a white T-shirt. But there was the glimmer from his Swiss-made watch that gave him away. I had never seen him so cheerful before.

"Why would we have a hard time getting here?" was Yvan's reply. "You gave me directions and I have GPS."

"I don't know, Yvan," said Maxime. "I'm just glad you made it. Really glad you made it."

Yvan told Maxime that he wanted go back up to the room if dinner wasn't ready, and we began to walk away. But before we did, Maxime pulled me close to him by my forearm and said: "Did you do it yet?" I pulled my arm away and walked out of the room with Yvan. Back in the upstairs room, Yvan and I stood in silence, but only for a few moments. After a while I walked towards him and he opened his arms to me.

"What's wrong?" he asked.

"I should be asking you that," I told him. "You don't look at happy."

"I'm thinking about leaving the seminary," said Yvan.

"No, you're not."

"I am," said Yvan.

"I don't want you to leave the seminary."

"It's not up to you."

"You don't know what you're saying. You're not thinking clearly."

Yvan's laugh was mirthless.

"I don't see why it should matter to you," he said.

"Did you quit boxing for good when you lost a match?" I asked Yvan.

"But I never lost a match and it's not the same thing. And what does that have to do with anything?"

"You're acting like you've just been defeated. And to think that it was Maxime that did it."

"Maxime hasn't done anything. And as I said before, if I leave the seminary or not, it has nothing to do with you."

"It does. I don't want to be the reason why you never became a priest."

Yvan told me that he didn't care what I thought, and I asked him why.

"Because I'm not sure I can trust you," Yvan said.

"Oh God, here it comes."

"What did Maxime mean when he asked you if you had done it yet?" Yvan asked, pulling me towards him.

"That's not what he said," I replied, yanking myself away.

"Yes, it is. I heard him."

"I don't know what he meant. Why don't you trust me?"

"Because you came out of nowhere and I'm realizing that I don't know anything about you. It's strange. You could be a murderess. You could be plotting to kill me."

"Really, Yvan? A murderess. No one uses that term anymore. That's like something out of a black and white movie with Bette Davis."

"Are you?"

"Am I what?

"A murderess?"

"No."

"Are you married?"

"You already asked me that."

"No, I didn't," said Yvan. "Bernard did."

"No, I'm not married," I said. "And I'm going for a walk."

"Where can you go dressed like that? You're not wearing the right shoes."

Yvan looked down at my feet and noted the ballet flats that I wore. He'd caught me unawares when he'd come to the house earlier, and I hadn't put on proper shoes. Yvan sat on the edge of the bed sullen, and I muttered something about taking a walk around the house. I told him that I'd be careful and wouldn't come back with frostbite. I left the room. In the window in the hall, I saw a bird alight on the sill. It was a magpie, and as they were birds with minds fixated on revenge,

I wondered what it wanted. I walked the flight of stairs up to the third floor, where we weren't supposed to go as it was the staff floor. Suddenly the walls were narrow and it felt like I was in someone else's house and I shouldn't be there. The walls were papered in old, reddish-brown wallpaper, which set the walls here apart from the wood paneling in the rest of the house. It was clear that this part of the house was meant for servants. At the end of the hall was a room with a shorter door than the others, like a room where a troll would live. I turned the knob expecting that it would be locked, but it wasn't.

I walked into the room and was surprised to find it already lit. The walls were covered in photographs and newspaper articles that had been Scotch-taped to the wall. All the items on the wall prominently featured Yvan's face, which had become as recognizable to me as my own face. There was a picture of Yvan with a bloodied nose. There was a picture of Yvan standing with his training partners after winning an exposition bout in New Jersey. There was another picture of a bloodied Yvan, but in this one he had a gash on the left side of his head and there was blood on his cheek and his upper lip. It was someone's violent male fantasy. There was Yvan winning an amateur boxing award and Yvan at a college formal with a pretty blond girl who had a face like silly putty: you couldn't really make out any discernable feature. There were personal pictures of Yvan, some of which included

Maxime, but not all. There was a picture of Yvan and Maxime together on the back of a jet ski somewhere in the Caribbean. Maxime sat behind and had his arms wrapped around Yvan's body.

Leaving Maxime's shrine to Yvan, I returned to the hall and made for the stairs to return to the lower level. By the time I heard the footfall of someone coming up the stairs, it was too late and I was already bumping into the person. It was the cook, Rhonda, and she said: "You weren't supposed to come up here. I told you not to come up here." I shoved her to one side, surprising even myself, and I descended the stairs.

I returned to the bedroom where Yvan was. He was standing in just his boxer shorts, not unlike one of Maxime's pictures from his shrine. Suddenly Yvan no longer felt like a person but someone's fictional idea of a person. He was like someone who could be taken away as quickly as he had appeared, like a toy your parents changed their mind about giving you. I wanted to cry.

"What's wrong?" Yvan asked.

"Why are you in your underwear?" I asked him.

"I took a shower," he said. "I didn't have any clean clothes so I had to put on some of Maxime's things. He has a whole drawer of stuff in here."

"You put on Maxime's boxers?" I asked Yvan.

"Dinner's ready," I heard Rhonda call from the hall.

Rhonda served the three of us at table, and I noticed that her fingernails had very well-done French tips. Maxime was seldom at the house so Rhonda and her cousin probably had the run of the place. She served us venison in a stew, and the buck heads hung up on the wall regarded us disapprovingly. Dinner turned out not to be beef after all. Maxime was very chatty during dinner, but I hardly remembered a word he said afterwards. It all had to do with himself and his own motivations even if it was specifically about me or Yvan. He was very good at not dropping any hints about the blackmail. As Rhonda was clearing the table when the dinner was completed, Maxime said that there was an isolated spot on the property that he thought Yvan and I should visit.

"It's late," said Yvan. "Charlotte and I need to be getting back. I think I'd better drop her off at her apartment."

"It's almost midnight, Yvan," said Maxime. "You can't be serious about going out now."

I checked my watch and it was 11:45. Yvan sullenly agreed to go with Maxime to this spot of his, and I agreed to go too. Maxime told us that it was on the far side of a lake and it could only be reached by a rowboat. The boat rest at the end of a path through the garden on a sort of small pier. Even in the night-time the environment here seemed very woodsy and secluded, like an isolated place upstate you'd be sent to for camp when you were 11. Every state had an upstate that people further south regarded with contempt. Yvan got into the boat first and helped me inside. It wasn't long before we were midway across the lake, which was larger than what you'd expect a lake on private property to be. It was dark and Yvan rowed the rowboat slowly and solemnly like it was our own funeral bier.

Maxime was brimming in anticipation as the rowboat collided with the land. A low cabin was close to the shore, so much so that we could see the pair of candles slowly burning their wicks inside. This must have been what Maxime was preparing for when Yvan and I got to the house. When we reached the inside of the cabin, Yvan and Maxime made small talk, spending a fair amount of time discussing the dean. Yvan liked the dean, but Maxime didn't. The cabin was like a single person's studio with a bed backing onto one wall and chairs and a couch close to the opposite wall. I wanted to sit in one of these chairs, but as I walked toward it, Maxime said: "No, Charlotte. Over here." He took me roughly by the arm and sat me on the bed.

"What are you doing to her, Maxime?" Yvan asked.

"Sit on the bed with her," Maxime shouted.

Yvan gave him a long, hard look, but followed his direction. I crossed my legs and Maxime laughed.

"She's wearing underwear this time," he said.

Yvan didn't laugh, but it was clear he took Maxime's meaning.

Maxime sat on the other side of Yvan from me, placing Yvan in the middle.

"Charlotte, raise your arm," said Maxime. "Let Yvan

see that feminine curve from the top of the chest to the armpit to the arm. Oh no. Looks like we've got a little bit of hair. That's not very feminine. How very human of you, Charlotte. I know I've got razors in here some place. Let me see."

Maxime found the razors in a drawer. He ripped open the plastic package of ten or twelve and handed one to Yvan. Yvan removed the plastic razor protector and placed it gently on the bed. "Be careful you don't end up lying down on that plastic piece later," said Maxime. Yvan raised my arm higher in the air and I swallowed in anticipation. "Wait, wait," said Maxime, and he handed Yvan a can of shaving cream, which Yvan sprayed under my arm. He shaved first under one arm and then the next. When he was done, he handed the razor and the shaving cream to Maxime.

"Now take your hand and place it on her knee," Maxime said.

"What?" Yvan asked.

Maxime took Yvan's muscular hand and placed it on my knee. I wondered if my skin felt as cold to Yvan's touch as his hand felt to me.

"Then take your hand and move it up from her knee to her thigh, pulling up the hem of the skirt with it," said Maxime.

Yvan complied, pulling up the hem of my skirt and exposing my left thigh in the stockings.

"It's like pulling teeth," said Maxime. "Continue to

use that hand to expose the thigh. Meanwhile, take the other hand and push it between her legs."

"Maxime, stop," I said.

"No one told you to speak," said Maxime. "You just lay there and do as your told, you lobster trap."

Lobster trap, now that was a good, old-fashioned insult. I covered my face with my hand and felt as Yvan explored under my skirt with his own. But then Yvan stopped and I uncovered my face to see that he'd stood up. Maxime stood up too and Yvan grabbed him by the shoulders and shoved him hard against the wall. Maxime got angry, angrier than I'd ever seen him, and he fought with Yvan. They struggled in the narrow confines of the cabin, knocking over things: the lamp and porcelain bowl on a table by the door, a mirror. When Yvan pushed Maxime roughly again, Maxime made a fist and jabbed Yvan hard in the mouth. Yvan hadn't been expecting that, and he first stepped back in shock before finally getting down on one knee. Maxime was taller than Yvan but looked slight and boyish in comparison to Yvan's muscular frame.

"Yvan, I'm sorry," said Maxime. "I didn't mean to."

"Get out," said Yvan.

"Yvan."

"Get out!"

Maxime gave the two of us a once over and then he left the cabin. As he didn't close the door when he left, Yvan used his foot to roughly kick it shut. It slammed so hard that the roof shook and dust particles landed on the bed.

"If Maxime takes the rowboat, we'll be stuck here, Yvan," I said.

"I don't care," said Yvan.

"I do. I have a shift tomorrow."

"It'll be all right, Charlotte," said Yvan.

He kicked off his shoes and lay in the bed. I gently pulled off my ballet flats and placed them in a corner of the room. They were white and I didn't want to dirty them anymore than I already had. When I joined Yvan in the bed, he pulled me close. He kissed me on the cheek, which though a childish thing to do was what I wanted at that moment. He began to undress himself: pulling off his sweater and shirt first, and then unzipping his pants. But I remained dressed, and we spent the night like that: with Yvan in his Hanes underwear and me still in my zipped-up dress.

13

DECEMBER 1, 2008

There was a cinema in town that charged four dollars to see old movies at the matinee hour. Yvan called me and suggested that we go as he thought we should talk. We'd decide what we wanted to see when we got there. At the ticket stand, the man at the counter listed the movies off to Yvan and me since the print on the board behind him was so small that neither of us could read it. They were playing *The Texas Chainsaw Massacre*, *Pet Sematary*, and *A Handful of Dust*, and I had to convince Yvan to see the last on the list. I'd watched the film a long time ago on a streaming site in college, and I always remembered the scene where Brenda, living alone in the apartment she'd taken for herself in the city, went outside and bought candy from a seller on the sidewalk.

After that Yvan suggested that we go to a cafe and

talk since we couldn't do much talking in the theater. Even if there hadn't been that college student talking throughout the movie and distracting us, we wouldn't have been able to have a real, honest conversation. And we wouldn't be able to see one another's faces in the menacing darkness of the theater. As a waiter delivered food to the couple sitting behind us, I thought how I'd never eaten with Yvan in a cafe. It was so unlike him. In all the months that I'd known him, we'd only once eaten in a public place. I thought Yvan was looking very dapper in his collared shirt and Aran sweater. But he must have been hot because after we ordered he unbuttoned the second button on his shirt. The first button had already been undone.

"I hope everything that's happened hasn't turned you off your lessons," I told Yvan. "You've been doing so well."

"I don't know how you can even think about that."

"What do you mean?"

"I don't think we should continue them," said Yvan. "That's the main thing I wanted to talk to you about."

"But the fall term isn't over yet," I told Yvan. "I don't want to be responsible for you failing your test. Here, translate this line. 'Et son bras et sa jambe, et sa cuisse et ses reins, polis comme de 'lhuile, ondoleux comme un cygne'."

"Listen, I've been taking copious notes and reading a lot of books since you started tutoring me, Charlotte. You won't be responsible for me failing my test.

I won't fail. And besides, it's like when I was boxing. You just have to know when it's time to quit."

"But we still have unfinished things between us, Yvan. I don't think you should act too quickly. Listen to me, Yvan. I'm very happy that I met you. You're like the bubbles I used to play with when I was a kid. My dad always used to buy this bath soap that made bubbles."

"Mr. Bubbles."

"And the shampoo that doesn't burn your eyes so it's safe for kids. They're just things that I remember from being a child, and when I'm with you I feel like I'm transported back to that place."

"Well, I'm leaving town for a few days," said Yvan. "I already told the dean that I had to go to LA for something."

"You're going to LA, Yvan? That's not like you at all."

"I know it's not like me, and that's why I'm doing it. I made up a story about how I needed to go to a friend's funeral. I don't know if the dean believed it, and I don't care. Maybe I'll sleep with a few prostitutes while I'm over there."

"Maybe you'll sleep with a few prostitutes," I repeated. "Now you sound like Maxime. Everything you're saying sounds ridiculous to me."

"I don't care how it sounds to you," said Yvan. "Maybe I'll see you when I come back. Maybe I won't."

After Yvan left me at the cafe, I didn't want to go

to back to the apartment so I wandered the streets.
I thought I'd buy candy and imagine myself in the
midst of an aristocratic decline like Brenda in *A Handful of Dust*, only it would just be a lie since I wasn't
anything like her. It's funny because it always felt
like Brenda was the central character and not Tony.
But I never found any street salesman selling candy
during my walk, and I soon was distracted by the gar-
bage men who should have been picking the trash up
from the street-side but instead would stop to talk to
p3opl3 on the sidewalk that they knew from outside
of work.

I walked past the open door of a church where the
preacher was actively engaged in a sermon from his
place on a stage. I wasn't in the mood for a sermon just
then, but a woman was walking in with her husband
and it made me think of the seminary because the
husband was fingering a crucifix around his neck. I
walked in and found only a handful of churchgoers in
attendance. In a corner of the room a man cradled his
pet chinchilla. The light in the church was blindingly
white and modern, and the preacher in his honeyed
voice was saying: "And I will make them eat the flesh
of their sons and daughters, and they will eat one
another's flesh during the stress of the siege imposed
upon them by their enemies who seek to take their
lives," which he told his listeners was written in the
book of Jeremiah.

On the way back to the apartment, I stopped at

the store to buy groceries. The plastic grocery bags rustled as I scaled the stairwell in my apartment building, and I didn't hear a peep from anyone. In my apartment, I considered what I'd have for dinner and it suddenly occurred to me that I was angry that Yvan was leaving so suddenly. The phone rang and I walked from the kitchen into the living room to answer it. It was Luc and he made some ridiculous remarks about a dream that he had, which I quickly forgot. After I got off the phone with him, I noted that there were sounds coming from the apartment below. The couple arguing were so heated that they even banged on the ceiling of their apartment with a blunt object. It must have been the top of a broom. I opened the door out into the hall because I couldn't make out the words of the bellicose couple, and I was curious to know what they said to one another and whether it was worth the fuss. Door opened, I realized that there were two arguments taking place: one argument involving the couple downstairs and a second argument emanating from Shannon's apartment. I slammed the door, though I couldn't say why just then. Closing my eyes, I heard the rush of the water in the canal behind St. Vincent's that had carried logs to the mill in former days. The canal builders hadn't intended it to be a tranquil waterway, but it seemed so to me then.

A week later, I was in the kitchen putting the leftovers in Tupperware containers. Tupperware or Rubbermaid, I can't remember. I put a piece of chicken that I was half finished snacking on down, and I returned to the living room. As I was walking, I heard a knock at the door and turned around. Opening the apartment door, I discovered two uniformed police officers. They informed me that I'd better take a trip down to the police station with them, so I should drop whatever I was doing. I complied without any back talk, as my father would say. "I don't want any back talk," he would tell me. Grabbing my coat, I followed the officers out of the apartment. It was only as we three were descending the stairs that it occurred to me to ask them what they wanted me for.

"Shannon Bertin in 3H was found murdered this morning," said one of the officers.

I stopped walking and the officer said: "Keep it moving, Miss."

At the station, the officers led me into an interrogation room, though I only had to answer questions from the one. The other officer left and presumably went about his business: probably writing tickets for various real or imagined infractions. There was no window looking into the interrogation room from the hall as there is in the movies. The officer asked me a series of mostly-to-the-point questions about Shannon and my neighbors in the apartment building. He asked me whether I'd been in Shannon's apartment before, and I told him that I had. He asked me where I'd been on the night of the murder, which was the night before, and I told him that I had gone to Lino's, a restaurant outside of town. I'd come home very late. The officer nodded and muttered something about how Shannon's body would already have been found by the time I returned home. He was done with me and ushered me from the room.

The police station wasn't close to the apartment building as the one station seemed to serve the whole Western part of town. It had begun to rain, so after leaving the station I settled on taking the bus home rather than walk, which is what I typically have done. The bus shelter was across the street from the station, and behind it was a gas station with a 24-hour convenience store. As I sat in the bus station, I watched the clouds crash together in preparation for a storm and I noted how the declining light caused the telephone poles to cast violet shadows on the ground. A man sat beside me in the bus shelter, but he didn't say anything to me.

The bus came and the man sitting beside me in the bus shelter followed me on. He sat across from me, opening a package of candy corn that he'd bought from the convenience store behind the bus station. Yvan had a sweet tooth and candy corn was one of his favorite things, so I was reminded of him. Without thinking, I must have smiled at the man because he winked at me and rubbed his mustache in a suggestive way. I turned away from him, towards the window where I noted how the telephone poles were spaced at regular intervals. From the window, I saw the men coming home from the lumber mill. The thud of their boots and their chatter couldn't be heard, but I could imagine all those things. Although their faces were bent towards the ground sullenly as they walked along, when one of their friends spoke to them they smiled and became themselves. I pictured them all wearing silk boxer shorts like I'd seen Yvan wearing in one of Maxime's shrine pictures.

When I reached the apartment, I opened all the windows because I liked how the wind felt before a storm: riled up and spurred on by the cold. I wanted to take a shower, but all I could think of for some reason was Maxime taking pictures of me with his camera. The urge to call Yvan washed over me in waves. I suddenly felt that I needed Yvan beside me or at least I needed to know where he was. Somehow I felt closer to him than I'd ever felt before. There was no dial tone when I picked up the apartment phone, so I hung it up and tried again. The second time I had a dial tone and I punched the buttons for Yvan's room at the seminary. The call was answered, but it wasn't Yvan. It was his roommate, Ulysse, whose existence I had forgotten about though I'd heard mention of him many times. I'd even seen him before as Yvan had pointed Ulysse out to me at the seminary one time. Ulysse had been walking to class at the time.

"Sorry, Ulysse," I replied to Ulysse's inquiry about how I was. "I was looking for Yvan. I thought he'd be home."

"Hold on a moment," said Ulysse. "He's right here."

I gasped softly as Ulysse called to Yvan in the bunk bed. That's how I imagined it: Ulysse sitting at the desk and Yvan reading in the lower bunk. I also imagined that Yvan had another pair of boxing gloves hanging from a pole of the bunk as well as posters of dead boxers on the wall. I imagined these things though I'd never been to Yvan's room in the seminary. Only family members were allowed.

"Hi, Charlotte," Yvan said sedately after he'd been handed the phone receiver.

"I didn't think you'd be back already."

"I am," said Yvan. "I got back yesterday."

I told Yvan that I wanted to see him. Shannon had died and the police thought it had probably been Kurt that had done it, but I knew it was probably Rutherford. I had seen Shannon in passing a few weeks prior and she'd told me that Rutherford was getting out on a technicality. Yvan and I had talked about Rutherford before, he knew his story, and I wanted to get his opinion about it. Really, I just wanted to see Yvan. There's a scene in the book that I wrote where the protagonist calls the man she's been seducing on the telephone after something bad happens. Yvan suddenly became attentive as if he'd been lying down before and at that moment sat up.

"I didn't tell you this, but when I was younger I wanted to join the French Foreign Legion," Yvan said.

"My parents wouldn't let me. My mother was still alive then. This was before I went to college."

"I think you told me that before," I told him.

"No," said Yvan. "I couldn't have. It's something that I never tell anyone because it seems so stupid now. I guess I should apologize for what I said before. About LA. I didn't do any of the stuff I said I would do. I can't say it out loud because Ulysse is in the room. Yes, Ulysse. I trust you. Mind your own business. Anyway, I think you know what I mean. I just needed to get away. All I could picture were the men walking to and from the lumber mill and the mill catching on fire. Maybe I felt like I was on fire."

"I have a question I need to ask you," I said. "You should just say yes or no."

"All right," said Yvan.

"Are you a virgin?"

"Yes."

I didn't say anything to that, but somehow I knew. In my book the seminary student, Julian, is a virgin. It's meant to be a surprise because everything about Julian gives the impression that he's slept with heaps upon heaps of women. Yvan filled the growing space of silence with small talk like stuffing packing peanuts into a box. The talk just seemed to rattle around. At the end of it all, Yvan told me that he had a doctor's appointment the next day, but he'd be able to meet me in two days, which was a Tuesday. Tuesday

seemed like a point perilously far into the future, but
I agreed.

14

DECEMBER 2008 – JANUARY 2009

And then I got a call from Linda at the diner who asked me if I wanted to go ice skating before our shift. On Mondays we worked the 10 to 6, and since I wasn't meeting Yvan then I had no reason to refuse. It made sense to go ice skating in the morning and on a weekday because it was unlikely that there'd be many people at the rink. I had my ice skates safely in a box stuffed under my bed. There wasn't much room in the closet. Walking into the bedroom, I got down on my knees and reached for the box. I brushed away the thick, loculated tufts of dust that seemed to penetrate every corner of the apartment. It made me think of visiting my grandmother at her large house in Connecticut and the mountains of dust there because she didn't like housekeepers coming into the house to clean. She didn't trust them. Sherry sits up attentively at this, but not because she's surprised that my grandmother didn't like housekeepers. She's surprised that my grandmother had a mansion in Connecticut. She doesn't tell me this, but her face says it all.

I met Linda at the ice rink and was surprised to find her wearing a beautiful mink coat. It wasn't full length but came down to just below her waist. You could tell it was high quality fur because the hairs were long and soft rather than short and prickly. Linda was like an '80s B movie actress, and part of me wondered what Yvan would think of her. He rarely came to the diner to eat, though I told him he was welcome. I'd mentioned Yvan to Linda before, but only in response to her questions because she told me that she'd seen me with a really butch guy who looks like a graduate student. I didn't think Linda was the sort of person who would deliberately steal your man from you, but she's very pretty and people can be opportunistic.

There were more skaters at the ice rink than we were expecting, but it was nice weather and it was still pleasant to take an unexpected skating trip. It was just something different and out of the ordinary. The younger skaters were being boisterous as they didn't know how to skate properly and were incessantly colliding with one another or falling over. Linda said: "I don't know why there are so many high-school-aged people around on a weekday." But then I reminded her that private schools got out a little early in December and Christmas was on Saturday, which was less than a week away. Linda complimented me on my beautiful skates and was shocked to learn that I used to be a semi-professional ice skater. The skates are made from thick red leather and look new as I'd had them professionally repaired after I gave up ice skating for good. Skates like these are very expensive as are the lessons that I'd taken as a girl. I did well enough regionally and made it to national competitions, but I never did well enough to travel to Europe for international competitions, which is what I'd wanted. Linda thought it would be funny to loop our arms together and skate across the outdoor ice rink as if we a couple, so that's what we did. The high school students thought we were lesbians and gawked at us in awe, which Linda seemed to enjoy.

Linda's older than me, and she has a mature sensuality that meshes well with her unusual face. We spent more time at the rink than we should, and by the time we took our skates off and got into Linda's car, we only had five minutes to make it to our shift on time. Linda didn't care. She said that Harry, the manager, couldn't fire both of us. Harry didn't own the restaurant. It was owned by a woman named Mary Rathouser, who we all assumed was Harry's wife.

When I reached home after my shift, I discovered a message from Yvan on my voicemail. He said he was calling from the doctor's office where he'd gone to have a checkup and to try a new experimental medication for his Sweet Syndrome. This syndrome was something he'd brought up before but had always seemed to minor. I felt an urge to see him, so I called a cab and hurried to the doctor's office, which was in a non-descript complex on the outskirts of town. Entering the doctor's office, I didn't see any sign of Yvan in the waiting area, and it occurred to me that I'd probably missed him. He might even have driven past me in the parking lot outside as I was being dropped off in the taxi. But then the door to the examination rooms in the back opened, and I was met with the familiar figure of Yvan. He looked more tanned than usual, which jibed with his story of just getting back from LA.

A female tech was administering a survey to a patient in the waiting area as I approached Yvan. He was shaking the doctor's hand, and he nodded at me when he saw me. The doctor told Yvan that he ought to go to the nurse's station to pick up his medication, and the doctor handed him the script that he'd penned. Even seeing the prescription briefly, I recognized the rushed, sloppy hand of a physician who'd long been in practice. After Yvan walked away, I remarked to the doctor that it was nice that Yvan could pick up his medication here rather than have to drive to the pharmacy.

"It's a medication with provisional approval by the FDA so that's why we keep it in the office," the doctor said. "They wouldn't have it at the pharmacy."

"Oh, right," I said. "I hope Yvan's okay."

"The medication should help," said the doctor. "His rash will be gone in no time. It's just on his shoulder, and I don't see any reason why it shouldn't be gone in two weeks."

"It probably didn't help that he took that trip to California."

"No, but I'm not too concerned."

"And you're not concerned that he has something more serious, like leukemia?" I asked.

"We do have that concern, but we'll wait and see how he does on the medication. His overall health is good. His CBC is a little off, but not like we would typically see in an acute leukemia case. We can get a bone marrow sample if the symptoms don't improve, or in the off chance that symptoms get worse."

Then Yvan returned, playfully rattling the bag of his medications in front of my face. We both smiled and said goodbye to the doctor. Yvan drove me back to the apartment, and I suggested he come inside. He asked me if I was sure, and I told him that I was. Of course, I was. I made dinner and we sat and ate in front of the switched-off television. Yvan said he had a headache and didn't want to eat with the television on just rattling nonsense in the background. That's what he thought anyway. At this point it was after 10 in the evening. The telephone rang and as I stood there staring at it, Yvan asked me why I didn't answer.

I said: "It's Maxime."

"You don't know that," said Yvan.

With a sigh, I picked up the phone. "Hello?" I asked.

"I thought you'd be home," said Maxime. "Is Yvan with you?"

"Yeah," I replied. And then turning to Yvan, I whispered: "It's Maxime, like I told you."

"I haven't seen him since he left town," Maxime continued. "I stopped by his room this afternoon, but his roommate said that he was at a doctor's appointment. I hope he's okay. Anyway, I think I should stop by."

"I don't think you should."

"Well, I'm across the street, remember," and Maxime laughed. "We're not quite done yet, Charlotte. I'll be over in a few minutes."

"What is it?" Yvan asked as I hung up the phone.

"It's Maxime," I said. "He's coming over."

"Damn it. Don't let him in when he buzzes at the front door. No, no. Let him in. We'll listen to what he has to say."

Yvan switched the television back on just seconds before Maxime rung the buzzer to get into the building. I sigh because it occurred to me that Maxime might have been standing outside on his cellphone when he called. Looking through the peephole, I examined Maxime. He wore an expensive leather jacket, and he looked more put together than usual. It wasn't that Maxime looked bad usually, it was just that his monomaniacal obsession with Yvan made him unattractive.

And as I got to know Maxime better I started to notice the paranoid elements of his personality. Maxime was good-looking and sturdily built. He was pretty pale typically, but on that day it looked like he'd been out in a warmer climate recently, like Yvan. Maxime had a wavy-brown cowlick that was longer than the rest of his hair.

"I hope I'm not interrupting anything," Maxime said after I'd let him in.

"You are," I remarked.

"I haven't seen you in a while," said Yvan.

"I know," said Maxime. "How have you been?"

And the two men shook hands as if nothing untoward had ever passed between them. Maxime sat across from Yvan at the small table in the living room, in the seat where I'd been sitting before he'd knocked. That meant that I had to stand.

Maxime asked: "So are we gonna do this or what?"

Yvan's face completely changed.

"If you mean that you'll watch while Charlotte and I sleep together, that'll never happen," said Yvan.

"You mean I came all this way for nothing?"

"If that's what you had in mind, then yeah," said Yvan. "You can just leave. Did you forget that we're both studying to be priests?"

"I didn't forget. It seems like you're the one that forgot. But you were never cut out for the priesthood, were you? You were a boxer, and you've got this sex appeal thing. You walk into a room and the girls are wet in a few seconds. I exaggerate, but you get the idea."

"Get out."

"But I just got here."

"And if you plan to leave with all your teeth, you'll head right on back to your house."

"Now, come on, Yvan. That's not like you."

"I know it's not like me," said Yvan.

"You've never been one to resort to violence, at least not outside the ring. Didn't Christ turn the other cheek?"

"Yeah, and it wasn't an ass cheek either. Beat it."

"It wasn't an ass cheek," Maxime said and laughed. "Now, Yvan, I think you've been watching a little too much late night cable. You should spend more time on your studies. Oh, Charlotte, you'll be glad to know that Yvan took his last French test this morning, so we ought to find out how he did soon enough. Fingers crossed."

"You actually came here because you wanted to watch us sleep together?" I asked.

"Yeah," said Maxime. "And don't forget what I have on you."

"Get out, Maxime," Yvan said, standing up finally.

Yvan walked over to his friend and shoved him. Maxime walked backward until he backed against the door to the apartment. Even with Maxime cornered, Yvan punched him hard in the jaw and Maxime crumpled into a ball on the floor. I'd never seen him so helpless, but the victory was a small one since it seemed to come at a price to Yvan. Something about Maxime's actions and words chipped away at Yvan. It was like he was already starting to change.

"Don't forget what I have on you," Maxime shouted from the floor. He swept away the blood and sweat on his face with the back of his hand.

"You don't have anything," said Yvan. "When I got back on Saturday, I went straight to your house while you were out. One of your roommates let me in. I walked right into your room and found your camera and all the pictures. Those fucking disgusting pictures of Charlotte. You should be ashamed of yourself. I couldn't even look at them. I didn't know what was on the other cameras so I took the rolls out and destroyed them."

"Fucking shit," said Maxime. "Fuck you."

"You wish, asshole," said Yvan.

Maxime made a ridiculous remark about how he'd done it all for Yvan and left the apartment. That was the last we ever heard of Maxime. I saw him occasionally, but he was like a stranger. After that, Yvan said he was tired and suggested that we go into the bedroom. We undressed and laid in the bed together. The apartment was totally quiet except for the sound of the rain lashing against the windowpanes. The rain had returned.

"Do you want to sleep with Maxime?" Yvan asked while we were in bed.

"How can you ask that?"

"Maybe you think he's horrible, but that doesn't change anything," said Yvan. "You might still want to sleep with him. You might find him attractive."

"I don't," I told Yvan.

"You don't what?"

"I don't find him attractive and I don't want to sleep with him. Is that what you think of me, that I just go around sleeping with whoever?"

"No."

Yvan got up to turn out the light and then he returned to bed. In the darkness, I couldn't see the rash on his shoulder from the Sweet Syndrome, although my eyes were still in the process of adjusting to the darkness. The rash would heal soon enough, I knew. Yvan had never been anything other than someone healthy to me, and I couldn't take the Sweet Syndrome seriously. This syndrome wasn't supposed to be in my story anyway so it was impossible to take it seriously.

Sherry asked me if that was Yvan and I's first time together, and I told her it was even though I thought it rude of her to ask. Yvan stayed with me in the apartment until a quarter to 10 the next morning when I went to the diner because I'd picked up the shift of another waitress, Rita, who couldn't work that day. Rita had a baby shower to attend. The town was quiet as I walked to the diner. The car drivers didn't honk their horns and there was no shouting from the windows. I thought I could hear the sound of the water sloshing in the canal that ran behind the town and ended at the mill in the outskirts.

Several millworkers walked into the diner just as my shift was starting. They pulled off their work gloves and sat in pairs at the bar. They must have been stopping in for breakfast before the start of their shifts at the mill. To me they had a way of speaking to one another that was all small talk: they never seemed to say anything important. It was a few hours into my shift that the cook told me I had a call. By then, Linda had started her shift so I was no longer working the diner floor alone. Linda agreed to cover my tables while I answered the phone. I knew it would be a member of Yvan's family on the other line calling about him, but I didn't expect it to be his father. Yvan's father loomed like a monstrous god in our lives. Even Yvan's voice grew quiet when he mentioned him. He was like someone that could swoop down from the sky and eat us at any time like how the old gods used to eat their children. He was someone who was occasionally spoken of but never seen: just an anonymous person of importance who was actually too important to be visible to us.

I suppose as far as he was concerned serious matters had arisen. I don't know if Yvan told his father that we had slept together, but I formed the impression that they'd spoken about it. With his deep, commanding tenor, Yvan's father asked me how I was, and then he wanted to know if things between Yvan and me were serious. To my surprise, Mr. Prevost seemed pleased that they were, or at least that I thought they were. "Would you consider marrying Yvan if he asked you?" That was Mr. Prevost's next question. I could hear the sound of customers coming in and out of the diner behind me and the cook shouting angrily about the food getting cold. I picked up the phone and ducked into a corner by a storage closet. The phone cord was long enough. I sat at the windowsill and watched the traffic race by outside the diner. Sometimes the drivers leaned their heads out of their cars to shout at one another. I told Mr. Prevost that there was no question that I would marry Yvan if he asked. Mr. Prevost was silent for a time.

Before the wedding, I was invited to meet with some of Yvan's relatives, and Yvan told me that his family had mutually decided to formally welcome me into the family so I wouldn't feel like an outsider. I wasn't meeting with Yvan's father, who was out of town on business, but with Yvan's maternal aunts as well as some of their relations and friends. Evidently, one particular aunt was wealthier than Yvan's father and it was important to have her approval. This aunt lived in a neighboring county and very much in the woods. I didn't know the area well, but I had the vague idea that she lived in a community of spread-out estates rather than the typical houses you'd find in a town. Renting the nicest car I could find, I began the hour-long journey. I was perhaps twenty minutes away from the house when I first heard the boom of shotguns blasting. The hunters had come out. There were rules about when hunters could chase certain prey, but I was old enough to know that people said "Screw the rules" and did what they want, especially people like I soon understood Yvan's maternal family to be.

Yvan's father had transformed himself by inter-marrying with them. They were French-Canadian too but already had money when they came here. The country road meandered through the forest without any habitation in sight. Although spring had come, the sky was dark as it had rained that morning and the heavens were yet to break out into sunshine. They never would that day. I heard the chirp of the larks in the trees as I drove with the window down; I heard the flittering of bird wings. I increased the speed of the car on the two-lane road as I didn't want to be late. I was supposed to reach the house of Yolande Barry, Yvan's aunt, in time for supper. I'd given myself adequate time to reach her house from the town, but I'd stopped at a gas station to buy coffee and then I'd had to stop at another gas station to use the ladies' room. So I increased the speed of the car and watched as the dial on the odometer went to seventy and then eighty. The road was just then turning a bend, and I didn't have any cause for concern about hitting any-one as I hadn't passed a single vehicle on the country road since I'd joined it after exiting the interstate. But as I turned the bend in the road, I suddenly became aware of someone standing in my lane. I jabbed hard on the break, so much so that the light fixture on the roof of the car dislodged and struck me on the head.

But I was more concerned about the man in the road. I hadn't hit him, but in his fright he seemed to stumble. Ater I collected myself, I noted that he was still sitting in the road. I pulled the car over and stepped out. Approaching the man, I realized he wasn't in his right mind. "Oh, thank you," he said, as I helped him to his feet. I escorted him to the roadside, thick with woods.

"Don't go there," the man said when we reached it.

"What's that?" I asked.

"You're going to the Barry's," the man continued. "Don't go. I'm related to them. They're all terrible, terrible people. You'll lose your mind if you marry into that family. That's what your doing, isn't it? You're marrying one of the sons of Jean-Louis. Don't do it. I would know, wouldn't I? I know them better than you. You don't believe me? Ask to meet some of the other family members, if they'll let you. They're not all pretty and rich. They're freaks. They hide the freaks."

Once the man was safely away from the road, I returned to the rental car and continued on. I disregarded what he'd said as I didn't have any objective other than to marry Yvan. I seemed drawn to the mansion by some magnetism. The sharp turns in the road became more severe just as the roads grew denser. I came across another sharp turn and though I had reduced my speed, I wasn't able to prevent myself from colliding with a deer. It struck the car front with a thud that jolted me. I pulled the car over again and approached the deer, It slowly died with my palm against its face. I felt as the life passed out of its body. In the book I wrote, the protagonist hits a deer with her car before she marries the seminary student.

When I reached the mansion, I was all in a muddle. A maid took me to a sitting room where Yolande and her sister Marie-Ange were. Yolande was a woman in her 50s with chestnut hair and night-blue eyes. She was skeletal and confined to a wheelchair. But her face was heavy with makeup, her hair appeared professionally styled, and her clothes were European. I formed the impression that Marie-Ange was probably younger than Yolande though she appeared older. Yolande had a way of occasionally barking orders at Marie-Ange: commanding her to fetch this or that, or to tell Marie-Ange to inform the cook that she'd changed her mind and wanted tiramisu for dessert instead of cookies and cream ice cream. Yolande was the owner of the house, which the maid whispered to me as I was led in to meet the two sisters.

Yolande inspected me severely, but she smiled after she decided that it was better to be friends with me. Marie-Ange didn't smile much and was always very serious in her aspect. I noted once while talking to them that Marie-Ange had a small tattoo of a snake swallowing a man on her wrist. After sitting in a chair across from them, I explained that I'd struck a deer on the way to their house. I hadn't been speeding, but it just hopped out into the road suddenly.

Yolande laughed and said: "Happens all the time. Naturally, I don't drive, but practically all the guests that come here have run-ins with deer."

"It's true," said Marie-Ange.

"I think they should cull them better, but who am I to say," said Yolande. "As I said, I don't drive. I don't shoot either. Oh, I go out shooting with the rest of the family, but I just watch. Someone just plants my wheelchair near the others and I watch them shoot. I can't follow. One time, Jean-Louis handed me a rifle for me to shoot a buck, but I just laughed at him. I told him that I might shoot him by accident if he wasn't careful."

"She nearly did," said Marie-Ange.

"No, I didn't. Shut up." Then Yolande turned to me and said: "Marie-Ange is a journalist and any intelligent thought she has she commits to paper. There's nothing left for conversation."

"You don't have to be so shy, Charlotte," said Marie-Ange.

"No, you don't have to be so shy," said Yolande.

"So someone carries your wheelchair when the others go shooting?" I asked.

"Yes, it's nice to be carried by a strong male servant,"

said Yolande. "We used to have a lot more around the place compared to now. I'm trying to economize. Yvan and Bernard will inherit everything when I'm dead so I hope there's something to inherit."

"Affairs aren't that bad," Marie-Ange noted.

"No, they're not," Yolande agreed. "I made some bad investments with Jean-Louis's guidance. They failed miserably and I lost a lot, but of course, it's vulgar to talk about money. Is it true that you're from Connecticut, if you don't mind me asking?"

"I have family there, but I wouldn't say that I'm from there," I said.

"Right," Yolande. "I did read your book, Charlotte. It was a good read. The sort of book that doesn't really become decent until the end, if you'll excuse my saying so. It's simply written, but a very compelling psychological study. And I suppose you might call it a coincidence that the protagonist falls in love with a seminarian, which you yourself seem to have done. Life imitating art and all that."

Marie-Ange sat up higher in her chair and glanced out of the wide dormer window to which she was the nearest of all of us. "I didn't read it," she said with a sigh. "Yolande was hogging the book and I didn't have a chance to read." The two sisters then chatted about other things and their talk soon descended into an argument. That's what it was: chatter that turned into an argument. I remained with them for two days. During that time, this sort of interchange was common, where the sisters jumped headfirst into the abyss of an argument of which the cause was never clear to me and the culpability for which could also not be clearly placed. As I watched them, I noted how Yolande seemed to delight in taking Marie-Ange down a peg. Marie-Ange tolerated it stoically. Maybe when she returned to her room Marie-Ange screamed to let it all out. She took her treasured Easy-Bake oven from childhood and dashed it onto the floor. Yolande explained that Marie-Ange hadn't inherited any of their father's fortune because she'd dropped out of college to marry an immigrant from the Eastern Bloc. No one really uses the term Eastern Bloc anymore, but that's what Yolande said. Their father, Yvan's maternal grandfather, had cut Marie-Ange out of the will, but that hadn't stopped Yolande from inviting Marie-Ange over as often as she could, just to rub her face into the things she hadn't gotten.

"Whatever you do, don't meet the rest of the family," Marie-Ange said after we had finished our dinner. "At least not our side of the family."

Most of our conversation had taken place in the living room before dinner was served. Though I'd arrived late, it seemed that Yolande had already decided to delay supper since she hadn't been particularly hungry. Marie-Ange told me later that Yolande only ate one meal a day.

"Don't tell her that," said Yolande to Marie-Ange's remark about my not meeting the maternal side of

Yvan's family. "She'll think we're all freaks out sacrificing in the woods. As if I'd be able to participate in a human sacrifice in my chair."

"I've been telling her to get a motorized scooter for years," Marie-Ange remarked to me.

"But I don't want a motorized scooter."

"She thinks there's something plebeian about a motorized scooter."

"No, that's not what I think," said Yolande. "I actually like being able to wheel myself along, and when I can't I have a servant to help me."

"And thank god for the servants," said Marie-Ange. "Yolande wouldn't be able to live if she didn't have them."

Yolande tossed Marie-Ange an angry look. She took a sip from her tea, shakily holding on to the tea dish with one hand. Then she dashed the tea dish with the cup to the hardwood floor. "Someone come pick this up!" she barked nonchalantly.

After the maid had cleaned the shattered things, Yolande said: "Actually, Marie-Ange is out of luck as we do have another member of the family visiting tonight. It's late and he should have been here by now, but it's Jacques, Yvan's cousin. He's finished his dissertation a semester early, and I invited him to the house to celebrate. He hasn't been here in a year."

"He doesn't like it here," said Marie-Ange.

"That's not true," said Yolande.

We were served dessert in the living room, which

we had retired to after dinner. After dessert was finished, Yolande told me that the maid, Michaela, would show me to my room. We would meet again downstairs later as Yolande liked to smoke cigars in the study, which had been a custom of their father's that Yolande had continued. As the maid led me upstairs to my room, she told me that if I was curious about what had happened to Yolande, the answer was that nothing had happened to her. She'd undergone many tests under the guiding hands of doctors, but no one could find anything amiss with her. That's when the psychologists had gotten involved. She was diagnosed with a nervous condition. It was true that she'd fallen from her racehorse, but there'd been no broken bones, no internal injuries. She'd simply decided not to walk anymore. That had been 20 years ago.

More than anything, I thought it out of place for the maid to gossip with me and tell me everyone's business, so I didn't say anything to her when she'd brought me to the room finally. It was at the end of the central hall on the second floor. After the maid had shut the bedroom door behind her, I walked to the large window along one wall of the bedroom. It was a dormer window and not unlike the many other dormer windows in the house. There was a vase filled with fresh-cut lilies on the dormer window seat. There were vases filled with the selfsame flowers throughout the room and the house. These were the flowers Yvan had brought when he first came to my apartment, and

I wondered if he had told them about it. I surveyed the landscape outside the window: appreciating the walled-off secret garden and the lawn that fell gradually into the woods. Even in the far distance, I couldn't see any other houses. One was either very rich or very poor to live this, so far distant from everything and everyone. And when you lived so far from everything, you acquired strange habits or resurrected them.

"I'm sure Yvan's father told you about some particular customs in this family," said Yolande when I met her later in the smoking room. She was smoking a fat Havana cigar and enjoying immensely the smoke rings she blew out into the room, tossing her head back lazily.

"Let's not get into that," said Jacques, who was Yvan's cousin.

Jacques had been expected all evening, though I didn't finally meet him until I came down to the smoking room after being called by the maid. Jacques was the image of Yvan, as if they had been cut with the same cookie-cutter from the same dough. He was bulkily muscular with a muscular neck like Yvan, and he even dressed the same way: khakis, the heirloom Vacheron Constantin watch, understated but expensive shoes. These were the details that alerted the rich that they were among their own. Jacques's hair was the same color as Yvan's. His eyes were the same shade. He had the same masculine curve from the back to his waist, and then flaring out to his thighs.

The only point of difference was that Jacques wore his hair longer than Yvan did. Jacques also sported a bushy mustache. The similarity was disarming and I found myself returning to Jacques throughout the evening.

"There's no reason to scare her when the wedding's still months away," said Jacques.

"But I've already been told everything," I told Jacques. "I met with Yvan's father a few days ago and he told me everything. He even introduced me to some people who'd be at the wedding."

"Oh, so you met Dad then," said Jacques.

"I guess so, yes."

"You must think we're all so incredibly weird," said Yolande.

"Better not tell her about the magneto-mesmerist," said Marie-Ange.

"Pardon me?" I asked.

"My doctor believes I'd benefit from the experienced touch of a specialist from Europe," said Yolande. "Not my internist. My psychotherapist. This specialist calls himself a magneto-mesmerist or a magneto-hypnotist. I've heard both. Dr. Migliorati will be arriving in the States from Turin in two days actually."

"He's already here," said Marie-Ange. "He won't be coming to the house for another two days, but he's already here."

"You didn't tell me that," said Yolande, turning angrily to Marie-Ange.

"Yes, I did," said Marie-Ange. "You don't listen to me. You don't listen to anything I tell you. You only listen when I say it in front of someone else. Dr. Migliorati called me this morning and I told you what he said, just as I did now."

"It's your fault if people ignore you," said Yolande. "You should be more assertive. A meek photojournalist, Charlotte. Imagine that."

I laughed, but in a way that I hoped wouldn't upset Marie-Ange. Yolande and Marie-Ange began to argue again, and Jacques pulled me away gently by the elbow, much as Yvan would have done. He said that from the smoking room you could enter a terracotta-floored gallery that wrapped around to the back of the house. "There are foxes all around the woods here, and in the early morning you can see them darting out of their fox holes." I left the smoking room through a window that also served as a door. I allowed Jacques to lead me to the rear landing of the house, but the foxes were sleeping deeply in their holes.

It was late when I left Yolande, Marie-Ange and Jacques. The maid met me in the hall and escorted me up to the room like I was an imposter who needed an eye kept on her at all times. As if she thought I might steal the silver candelabra in the hall or the Turkestan rug. She silently followed me as I scaled the stairs. She opened the door for me when we reached the bedroom. Her goodnight wasn't sincere. In the room, I changed into the silk nightie that I'd brought with me. All the clothes I'd brought for the two-day trip had been bought shortly before setting out, driving to a town where there was a bevy of outlet stores. Nightie on, I raised the heavy bed covers and slipped under them. I couldn't sleep. It could've been that the bed was too comfortable or not comfortable enough. I heard the sound of a tree branch lashing against the window, and though it hadn't bothered me before it soon came to occupy my thoughts like a pool of blood rapidly expanding until it has touched everything in the room. Everything was red, red, red.

I heard footsteps in the hall. I opened the door a crack and watched as Jacques, dressed only in his underwear, tipped-toed down the hall to the bathroom. It was an old house, the walls were thin, and I heard the flush when Jacques was done with the toilet. Then I saw when he opened the bathroom door and returned to the hall. In the paltry light that came in through the hall window, I was startled by the resemblance between Jacques and Yvan, with Jacques seeming to emerge the better of the two.

15

JANUARY 7, 2009

Dr. Migliorati was already on his way to the house, which we learned at the breakfast table. I was sitting at table with Yolande and Jacques when Marie-Ange appeared and told us that she'd just gotten off the phone with the magneto-mesmerist. He had rented a car at the airport in Minneapolis and was on his way. Yolande concealed her alarm with a shrug and looked out the window. Dr. Migliorati arrived in the late afternoon before sunset. We were sitting in the smoking room which faced the front lawn and we saw him marching towards the house. I told Marie-Ange and Yolande that a man was approaching, and Marie-Ange said: "That must be him." He was tall and thin and looked very official in his Highland sweater over a starched white shirt and tie. But he was fashionably sans socks, which Jacques pointed out, and his shoes were too urban sophisticate for the country. Yolande and Marie-Ange received him coldly, as if they were intimidated by him, but there was still a sparkle in Yolande's eyes. The doctor surveyed the room as if he anticipated being asked to perform his magnetism right here, but Yolande said: "No, not here, Doctor. There's another room in the back. It's a room without windows, which I know is best." She told us that she'd read that a room without windows was ideal in order to prevent any magnetic forces from the woods and the lawn outside from interfering with Dr. Migliorati's technique.

Jacques wheeled Yolande out of the smoking room, and the rest of us followed. Dr. Migliorati was very quiet, and he seemed always to be making subconscious assessments of us. He was like the person on the airplane who sits quietly listening to their books on tape and never says or does anything to disturb anyone. The room was dark and Marie-Ange recommended that we light candles rather than flip the switch to turn on the ceiling lights. The maid was called, and she returned shortly after with fat, squat candles and matches. Marie-Ange was very pragmatic in her lighting of the candles, placing them in the four corners of the room and making sure the tables they were set on were sturdy so that they didn't fall over and set the house on fire. There was a chaise lounge in a corner of the room that Jacques wheeled to the center. He pushed a button, which made the chaise lounge completely flat so that Yolande could lie on it while Dr. Migliorati performed his procedure. Jacques joked that the last time he had visited the house, he had an argument with Marie-Ange and had been consigned to this chaise lounge for the night.

"Was it Marie-Ange?" I said. "You're sure it wasn't Yolande you had a fight with?"

"It wasn't a fight," said Jacques. "I just made her angry. And it was definitely Marie-Ange. I'd be surprised too if I were you, but when someone's pushed around they can snap at whoever's the easiest prey."

Marie-Ange shushed us, and our attention returned to Dr. Migliorati and Yolande. Dr. Migliorati had picked up fragile and slight Yolande from her wheelchair and was setting her down on the now-flat chaise lounge.

"Please be gentle, doctor," said Yolande. "Please."

The doctor laid her down very gently, cradling her head like an infant. Yolande's blonde hair was pinned back, and considering her age I figured she must have it dyed regularly because even her roots were an ice-cold blonde. I could see her roots from where I stood as the chaise lounge was relatively low to the ground, maybe only a foot or a foot and a half above the floor. Dr. Migliorati, who had mostly been silent in the short space of time that had elapsed after his arrival, suddenly appeared very active, muttering things to himself that the rest of us couldn't make out.

But I understood when he said: "It's a simple

technique involving the hands and the gaze. It's pain-
less, Madam."

"Thank you, doctor," said Yolande.

Marie-Ange asked if Yolande should remove her
double strand of pearls, and Dr. Migliorati said that it
didn't matter. Pearls didn't influence the magnetism.
He had already begun to place his hands on Yolande's
body, softly touching the fabric of her blue velvet
dress. He said that what Yolande wore didn't matter.
What was important was that she was still, quiet, co-
operative, and that the rest of us in the room didn't
make a sound. We occasionally heard the thud of the
maids feet as she paced outside the room, but other
than that we all endeavored to keep quiet as the
doctor demanded.

"Close your eyes and be at peace," said Dr. Migliorati to Yolande. "As if you were asleep."

He placed his hands on her shoulders and then
moved up to her neck, her temples, and the crown
of her head. Yolande became more relaxed, or so it
seemed to me. Her body had lost its stiffness. There
was the heat of a softly hissing radiator in the corner.
The doctor made several movements up and down
Yolande's body, generally beginning down at the feet
and moving up to the crown.

"I can feel it working," Yolande whispered, but she
said it loud enough that I could hear it.

Dr. Migliorati didn't say anything at first, but then
he said: "No. Several more treatments are needed. I'll

continue the treatments over the next several days. And we'll see how much function we can restore to the muscles and the nerves in your legs."

When he was done, Dr. Migliorati related to us an episode that had happened to him at the airport. He said he'd witnessed an irate passenger fight another person over luggage. Dr. Migliorati was smiling and genial as he related this story, and it seemed to me that we were being introduced to the real him. This version was different from the cold magneto-mesmerist that we'd first met. His body movements were more fluid and he seemed to move his head and his hands quite a bit when he spoke.

"Doctor, help me back into the wheelchair please," said Yolande.

Dr. Migliorati did as he was asked and he pushed the wheelchair this time rather than Jacques. He ambulated more quickly than Jacques had, which seemed to delight Yolande. At times, she reached back and gently rubbed his hands that gripped the steering poles of the chair. We didn't return to the smoking room but ventured instead to the dining room. It was too early for dinner, so we engaged in small talk. Yolande said that since Dr. Migliorati had a conference in New York it would be best if Jacques flew the doctor to Chicago where his flight departed from rather than the doctor having to drive in the rental car.

"I didn't realize you were a pilot," I said, turning to Jacques and smiling at him.

"I'm not," said Jacques. "At least not a commercial pilot. I just do it for fun. I have a pilot's license and I own an airplane. I'm a commercial law attorney, and I only fly when I've got the time. Residential-mortgage-backed securities."

"It's an easy thing for Jacques to drop you off in Chicago," said Yolande, resting her gaze on Dr. Migliorati. "All he has to do is fetch and fuel his airplane, which isn't far from here. He'll land it on the field we have in back of the house, and then someone will just have to return your rental car for you. Marie-Ange can do it or Charlotte. Or maybe Jacques can do it when he gets back. That way you can get to Chicago in time for your flight to New York, and you might even have a chance to see the sights. I'm sure Jacques will get you to Chicago quickly. Jacques just needs to figure out what he has to communicate to the international airport there so they'll allow him to land."

"Wouldn't it be easier to just take the bus?" Marie-Ange asked.

Marie-Ange had decided to be the killjoy of the party.

"Oh, don't be silly, Marie-Ange," said Yolande. "Why would Dr. Migliorati take the bus when he can be flown in a private plane by Jacques? Besides, it's the least we can do when he came all this way."

"Well, I'm sure there are things you're not anticipating with Jacques having to fetch his plane," said Marie-Ange. "I don't know what they are since I'm not a pilot, but permits, security clearances, things like that."

"Security clearances, Marie-Ange?" asked Yolande. "He's not flying to Saudi Arabia."

"Watch out, Marie-Ange," laughed Jacques. "Yolande is still trying to find a sultan and a harem for you."

"I've been trying to sell Marie-Ange into white slavery for twenty years," said Yolande. "No one wants her."

"Oh, there has to be a sultan somewhere who'll take her," said Jacques.

"I was thinking of Yvan," said Yolande turning towards me. "We all know here about this rash that he gets. This Sweet Syndrome. We know it's nothing serious, but his father tells us everything. You couldn't have found a better husband, Charlotte. I might say you're very lucky, if it's not too forward of me. But anyway, you're a beautiful girl and well-educated it seems. I've heard you have a master's degree."

"I have to agree with Yolande," said Marie-Ange. "Yvan has the sweetest character."

The sweetest character, they said. I'd begun to imagine Yvan's sweetness erupting in bumps all over his body.

"And tomorrow Dr. Migliorati will resume his magnetic treatment," said Yolande. "I'll need at least four treatments, so perhaps over the next two days you can double up. When do you have to catch that plane in Chicago?"

I didn't remain for the rest of Dr. Migliorati's stay. In fact, I drove away the very next day, which meant that I missed the opportunity of seeing Jacques land his four-seater airplane on the back lawn of the house. In the following weeks, I met with Yvan's father and Bernard again, but never at their house outside of town by the mill. Yvan's father told us a short time later that he didn't like the idea of Yvan leaving the seminary and getting married, at least not to me. He told Yvan that he wanted him back at the seminary, or if they wouldn't take him then he should go find a different seminary. There were others. He had no intention of paying for a marriage to me, although he'd previously agreed. But Yvan had already told the dean of the seminary that he wasn't going back and he'd also made all the preparations to be married. He'd found a priest willing to marry us. We'd done our interview with this man at his church although we ended up being married by someone else. I used to watch Yvan pace the room in the days before the wedding. By that time we were living together: in hotels and motels in the area. Yvan stole the reliquary of the apocryphal saint from the seminary church and sold it to pay for things we needed. It wasn't hard for Yvan to get back into the seminary church because everyone knew him and loved him. He was Yvan. I don't know what he did with the saint's femur. Maybe he threw it on the sidewalk somewhere.

"I have to," Yvan said before the theft. "I don't have any money and I don't want to ask Bernard. It's not fair to drag him into this."

At this point, with the story nearly over, Sherry rose from where we sat at the table. She returned to the hotel lobby and dealt with hotel business, but she wasn't gone for long. From the window, I watched a couple angrily walk out of the hotel. I guess they wanted to stay somewhere else. And when Sherry returned she said something that surprised me. She said that she'd love to continue our talks if I wanted to. I told her I would like that too. The story wasn't exactly finished. I didn't know where Yvan was just then or how much longer we'd be around. Yvan called from a payphone later and we agreed that I'd come down the next day in the early morning, presumably after Yvan had returned with all the things he needed. The early hour would suit Sherry since it'd be before the hotel got really busy.

When I came down in the morning, I found Sherry finishing up her breakfast in the hotel kitchen. I knew she'd be there since she'd told me she cooked her breakfast on the professional stovetop in the kitchen: fried eggs, Canadian bacon and toast with lots of butter. She shot up so rapidly when she saw me that she surprised me. She swallowed what was left of the food in her mouth and cleaned her plate. I shook my head and laughed. When she was done cleaning the plate, Sherry dried her hands with a rag as a sign that her morning ritual was done.

"You never told me if the magnetism worked and Yolande learned to walk again," Sherry said, turning to me.

"That's because I don't know," I told her. "Dr. Migliorati finished his treatments and Jacques flew him to O'Hare. I don't talk to them, obviously, after what happened. I got the impression that Jacques thought his aunt had always been faking it."

Sherry nodded. She'd reached the same conclusion. Then she asked me if I wanted to venture out onto the back lawn to try and catch the jackrabbits. It was still early enough to see them she said. They lived on the part of the lawn that sloped down toward the state land. The state land was mostly forested and even more unpeopled than the rest of the land in the county. Sherry told me that all kinds of people camped or hid out there, and I cringed at the thought that one day Yvan and I might be reduced to that. Camping out somewhere like fugitives. But I told Sherry that I would love to see the jackrabbits, and we marched out onto the back lawn through the kitchen door. Sherry had brought her jacket, but I hadn't thought to bring mine and I was cold. After about five minutes wait, we saw a jackrabbit. He was so small and fast that you didn't notice him at first. It was only when the jackrabbit had been sitting still for a while that you suddenly became aware of him. He'd been there for some time. When we returned to the house, Sherry asked me what was left of my story, and I told her that I hadn't described what happened after I had married Yvan. I figured she must be curious what our plans were. I also hadn't described the wedding. It'd taken place in a Catholic church on the roadside and I'd worn a donated lace veil. The priest knew a woman who was willing to donate the veil she'd been married in twenty-five years before. My dress wasn't white but beige. The church was dark and lit by candles since there was no electricity. The church hadn't paid the electric bill and the city had turned off the power. Our wedding had been like a movie I'd seen on TV once and because of that I thought it was quaint and didn't hold it against Yvan. As for as Sherry's question about the rest of the story, there was also the issue of the book I'd written and the relevance it had.

As I said that last part, we were taking our seats at the long metal table in the kitchen. Sherry looked at me long and hard, and then suddenly she glanced away. She said: "I think your book ends with you poisoning your husband. Well, not you, but the girl. Now that she has the guy, she loses interest." I didn't say anything in reply to that. I got up and walked into the pantry, which opened off the kitchen: sort of sitting in back of it and reached through a metal door. Yvan had told me that he'd left his gun in there in the event something happened and I needed it: in a shootout or a hostage situation, who knew. In addition to the gun, Yvan had hid other things like false identification, state maps, things like that. I removed the gun and returned to the kitchen. When Sherry realized what I held in my hands, she suddenly leapt up, but I managed to shoot her before she could get away.

16

APRIL 12, 2009

Sherry kept a small television in the kitchen. I turned it on and listened to a news story about a woman whose murder trial had excited many people in the local community. The journalists were all standing outside the courthouse along with interested locals, as typically happens in these cases. As the murderer came out of the courthouse after her hearing, a woman journalist ran up the courthouse steps to ask her why she did it and several other stupid questions, though I couldn't hear most of them over the commotion. The woman dismissed most of the questions she was asked, and the cameraman panned away to a second journalist who was discussing the trial at the sidewalk, at the very bottom of the courthouse steps. Meanwhile, scores of people continued to flock the streets. They were mostly huddled behind the second journalist delivering his broadcast while others stood under the shade of oak trees on the far side of the street. A billboard on the interstate behind them advertised locally-sourced lumber for hardwood floors. Then we went to Bambi's house.

On the television at Bambi's house, Yvan dances with his mother. He holds her closely and spins her around a few times. She's wearing a day dress and smiling, but she frowns when she learns that there's a girl at school that Yvan likes. He wants to invite her out somewhere. Her name's Lyla. Mrs. Prevost thinks this is a trashy name and she tells Yvan so. But then Yvan says maybe he won't invite Lyla to the movies since he's sure she likes another boy better. The boy is named Mike (most of the boys at school are named Mike). And since she likes Mike and not Yvan, Lyla would probably say no if Yvan invited her out anyway. Mrs. Prevost is satisfied with that and pulls Yvan closer. She kisses him on the lips and runs her hands down the back of his check shirt and into the seat of his pants. She turns to face the video camera that's seated atop a bureau and says, "Turn that thing off," but she's laughing as she says it. Yvan doesn't turn the camera off right away. He says, "Well, maybe I will say something to Lyla. I'll ask her if she likes popcorn and how much butter she likes on her popcorn." If she's the sort of person that likes a lot of butter or none at all. Yvan mentions that Lyla has a job after school, so maybe he'll meet her at the restaurant where she works, but that only confirms for Yvan's mother that she comes from the wrong kind of family.

The camera cuts to Yvan lying shirtless on bed. His torso and arms are tanned, and you can see the tan line along his waist because his jeans are pulled partly down. He's wearing jeans but not any underwear. Yvan's mother is sitting atop the bed too, comfortably atop the bed covers, but then she gets up to turn the camera off. A button atop the camera clicks the camera off and then there's the buzz of static. Yvan and I were sitting in the room in Bambi's house watching the old tape in a TV/VHS combo. Yvan was so happy when Bambi told us that there was a TV/VHS player in the room. I didn't know that Yvan carted old family tapes along with him until then. Sometimes Bambi came up to the room and looked in through a crack between the old, closed door and the wall. She didn't know that we could hear her plodding down the hall from her room. We'd been on the run for some time and I think I'd trained myself to hear footsteps since it was easy to hear Bambi's. She was pretty, but something about her was used up. Not just physically, but in her head. Rode hard and put up wet, as people used to say. It was Saturday at 10:20 PM when the VHS tape showing Yvan's closeness with his mother finished, and I wondered if he showed it to me because he wanted me to understand him better.

I wondered how Yvan's mother felt about him becoming a priest. If that was what she wanted for him or if she wanted something else. She kisses him sensuously on the lips in the video and she's always rubbing his arms and his body. She says in the video that she likes to go to the graveyard because it's quiet and she can do gravestone chalk rubbings there. Most people don't like graveyards so she can do her rubbings quietly and in peace. Once she took Yvan and he didn't enjoy it, but it was mostly because boys from school were there too and they were making a ruckus. As I watched Yvan's mother in the video, the thing that stood out most was her long hair. It came down past her waist and accentuated the feminine shape of her body. This hair always seemed to be falling on parts of Yvan's body, even when they were dancing. Like it was wrapping itself around him and pulling him toward her like tentacle suction cups. She wore these patterned dresses, like Diane von Furstenberg dresses, and there was something not-of-the-present about her. Maybe that's why Yvan liked her. Some mothers would pull their sons right back into the uterus if they could. I wondered why she'd never taught Yvan French and I never learned the answer from the tapes. When Yvan went to the bathroom, I rewound the tape to the scene where Yvan's mother is the prettiest. They're dancing. Yvan twirls her round and dips her body down low. She smiles elatedly at him and grips his arms tightly so she doesn't fall.

The next morning Yvan went to town for a grocery run, and Bambi knocked on the door to our room.

There were others renting rooms in Bambi's house so it could have been anyone, but I knew it was her. She wasn't wearing shoes, but I heard her walk. It was distinctive, as if you could discern Bambi's character from her walk alone. Rode hard and hung up wet. Bambi entered the room without knocking and she held a cigarette. She looked the room over, as if concluding that we hadn't kept things up the way she liked but hadn't decided when the right time to mention that to us was. She wore a floral-patterned dress and I was sure she'd be assaulted by insects when she stepped outside. "I hope you like the TV/VCR," she told me, finally deciding to acknowledge me. I sat on the edge of the bed, and I know I looked pretty because I could see my reflection in an old mirror beside the bureau. The mirror had acquired a tint from age, but I could still clearly see myself. A radio played hard rock music. "We love it," I told Bambi. She sat beside me on the bed and went on and on about nothing: about how everyone's smoking electric cigarettes, but she only likes Virginia Slims.

After I shot Sherry, I waited for Yvan to return to the hotel. I knew he'd be a while because he needed to lay low for the day since law enforcement had been alerted that he was in the area. As Yvan parked the car in the parking lot, Pierre Marie showed up in the hotel lobby looking for Sherry, but I told him I didn't know where she was. Pierre Marie was quiet. It was his nature to be quiet, but he seemed quieter than usual, and I was sure he suspected something. But he hitched up his tight pants and walked back up the stairs he'd just come down from. Pierre Marie lived up there in an apartment that was only accessible by the freight elevator. I was sure Sherry was still alive and Pierre Marie would find her later. After Pierre Marie left, I heard the sound from the television. There was a small TV playing behind the reception desk. A commercial was playing in which a mature man with shiny hair was standing beside a stick figure woman in a spaghetti-strap dress. They're standing in the bathroom. The man has just given himself a shave, and the woman wipes a long, pale finger along the sharp line of his jaw. She grins in satisfaction. The man turns to the camera and says: "For a shave that doesn't cut too close, choose Casanova Shaving Cream. I know she likes it and so will you," and he pulls the stick figure woman towards him.

It was an old TV and newer TVs were on the way. Televisions that were lifelike, where you could see all the pores on someone's face. Then Yvan returned. He entered the reception area where I was and said: "Let's go. You won't believe how difficult it was to get this car. The man only wanted to accept a credit card, but I only had cash. I told him that. Obviously, I didn't want to use my card because then they'd have my name."

"You could've used my card," I told Yvan. "I gave it to you."

"But that would be the same as me using mine since they're looking for both of us."

"No, they're looking for you."

"I don't know why you're angry, Charlotte."

"Anyway, what did you do?"

"I talked the guy into taking cash," said Yvan. "I told him I hadn't used a credit card since I lost my job. That's not exactly true."

"You're not much of a priest anymore, are you?"

"What's that supposed to mean?"

"It just means that you're completely different. I hardly recognize you."

Yvan said we should get as far away from that town as we could. The police had combed the area if the news reports could be believed. Eventually they'd realize where we were. Yvan asked me where Sherry was, and I told him I didn't know. "Let's go," Yvan said. "Now." He was sweaty and angry now, and I was right to say that he was completely different. He really was. There were lines in his face and all the sweetness was gone. Even the sweet marks from the Sweet Syndrome were gone. Even when he'd been a boxer, there'd been some gentleness there. I knew it from the photos I'd seen in Maxime's temple to him. Now Yvan was ruddy-faced with an angry red tan on the back of his neck. He had stubble coming in on the front of his neck, almost down to his clavicles. I left the hotel with Yvan, and he suggested I sit in the back seat. He thought it'd be suspicious if we sat beside one another in the car since he insisted they were looking for both of us. It was less suspicious if we didn't appear close: just a random man driving a woman somewhere. Yvan told me I shouldn't worry, and he laughed when he opened the glove compartment and found all the things that the prior owner of the car had left there. The men at the dealership had forgotten to empty the glove compartment. The last thing I remembered before I fell asleep in the back seat was all the horses we drove past after we crossed the state line. We came across the slope of a hill where horses were galloping in a team. We did see a man astride a horse behind the team, driving them, but as the horses didn't have brands and had a feral look to them, I assumed they must be wild horses. I couldn't see the face of the man astride the horse because the brim of his hat came down low and covered it, but I didn't picture Yvan's face. I pictured Jacques's face. By the time we entered Bambi's state and had settled into the room she let us, the rounded up wild horses would have already been branded by the Bureau of Land Management. Every state that has wild horses has a Bureau of Land Management to manage them.

Bambi didn't know what had happened to Yvan and me before we came to this out of the way place. Of course, she didn't or she wouldn't have rented the room to us. My life with Yvan, were it to go on, would be just fleeing from one out of the way place to another. After Bambi told me about the electric cigarettes, she mentioned she was going out of town for the weekend and asked if I would mind watching Travis and Gallipoli when they stopped by tomorrow. Travis and Gallipoli were her grandchildren. I nodded yes, that I wouldn't mind, even though I wasn't sure I'd still be around tomorrow. I didn't mind watching Travis and Gallipoli. We could play Monopoly and talk about Santa Claus. We could eat the reconstituted meat that Bambi had in the refrigerator. She couldn't afford steaks so she bought meat that looked like steak. Some people thought it tasted like steak too. After Bambi left the room, I heard her plod down the hall to her own apartment. Listening at the door to our room, I could hear her packing her things and grunting in anger when she couldn't find what she was looking for. Bambi left the house without saying goodbye, and I heard when she revved the engine of her Lincoln.

I walked to Bambi's apartment, which she left un-locked. The first room was a small sitting room with a couch and a window looking out onto the rose bushes in the back. Then there was a door in the bedroom and a second door into the bathroom. In front of the door to Bambi's bedroom, there was a table atop which was a white-gray Albuterol inhaler. It belonged to Bambi's adult son, who lived in another state. I opened the bedroom door and walked into Bambi's bedroom. In the center of the room was a waterbed draped in leop-ard print bedsheets. I knew it was a waterbed because

I was carried up in waves as soon as I sat on the edge of it. The thought of Bambi having sex here bothered me and I immediately stood up. From where I stood, I could see the Easy-Bake oven on the bureau and the white silk lingerie hanging from a hanger in the shoe rack in the closet.

Bambi didn't have a television set in her apartment, which surprised me. Earlier, after Yvan and I had first arrived, Bambi told me that she'd tried electric cigarettes, but she just couldn't get into them. I pictured her sitting in front of the TV trying to smoke an electric cigarette and then stomping her feet in frustration. Leaving Bambi's apartment, I walked down the stairs to the living room. In the room there was a large, ancient TV. It wasn't a TV/VCR combo, but it was connected to cable television. I used the remote control to turn on the TV, and it buzzed on to the news, where a woman was talking about a lamp she bought at a thrift shop which turned out to be worth $150,000. She explained that that was significantly more than what she'd paid for it. She seemed pleasant and the journalist interviewing her seemed pleased at her good luck. Everyone seems pleasant on television. In fact, I'd seen Yvan on TV months before I met him. When I saw him at the depossession party at St. Vincent's, I thought: "There he is. I found him." In the TV interview where I'd first seen Yvan, a journalist was asking him about a monastery that was being reopened out in the woods with help from seminarians at Yvan's seminary. Yvan seemed superhuman standing beside the man from the evening news hour. He was a seminarian, but he didn't seem like a seminarian at all. His voice was deep and masculine, and there was a strange confidence to him. He mentioned that he used to box, which surprised the journalist. Yvan's brown-blond hair was slightly curled in front and in his irises were scenes of him and me together over many endless summers.

It was raining when Yvan returned to Bambi's. I met him at the door, but he hardly looked at me. He seemed like a wet animal all drenched in rain like he was. His complexion was ruddy and bilious like a pimple, and when the rain dried as we scaled the stairs to our room, I saw the dense fair hair on his hands and on the back of his neck. I'd never noticed hair in those places before. The hair on his hands came almost down to his fingers. His nails were all battered and bent. Even his own mother wouldn't recognize him. She wouldn't want anything to do with him either. Yvan cradled a plastic bag under his left arm. When we reached our room, he opened the bag and took out a can of bug spray, cough syrup, and a teddy bear with shimmering terry-cloth hair untouched by the rain. "I wanted the non-drowsy kind but this was all they had," Yvan said about the cough syrup. He paused for a moment to cough and then he handed me the teddy bear. "I'm sorry, sweetie," he said. Yvan stumbled to the bed, and I saw that he was really and truly sick. I helped him with the child safety lock on the cough syrup, and as he drank it I told him that I had something better. I grabbed my purse and went downstairs to prepare the tea that I had been serving Yvan for several weeks. Even when we were on the run, I'd been serving it to him. When I reached the kitchen, I cleaned a spoon and then I removed the bottle of white pills from my purse. I took two pills and crushed them on the surface of the laminate kitchen counter with the spoon. Above the sink in the kitchen was a yellowed picture of a woman who I assumed must be Bambi's mother. A time stamp at the foot of the picture reported that it was taken in 1933. She was waiting for televisions to be invented. She had an expectant look on her face.

When the kettle came to a boil, I removed it from the burner. Then I picked it up and lowered the spout to pour the water into the teacup which already had the tea bag in it. I could hear Yvan coughing upstairs from all the way down here in the kitchen. I had to wait 5-10 minutes for the tea to cool or the heat would neutralize the active compound in the pills. The time passed quickly because I played with a microscope that Bambi had left on the kitchen island. She said that the former resident of our bedroom, a neurotic community college student, used to like to look at things under the microscope. I wondered what the girl would have thought if she'd looked at the life that Yvan and I had made together. If we'd be beautiful like I'd imagined us at first or if we'd be ugly, single-celled organisms. Perhaps she'd see the many endless summers Yvan and I should have had. Yvan was coughing louder than ever in the room, and I decided to put the crushed pills in and take the teacup up to him even though I didn't think the 10 minutes had elapsed. I scaled the stairs again, and when I reached the room Yvan was happy to see me though I knew the tea wouldn't make him any better. He didn't know I was the one making him sick. But Yvan was always clueless to malice, and he sat up cheerfully and drank the tea. I in turn grabbed the teddy bear with the lustrous hair that Yvan had bought and sat at the foot of the bed, pushing Yvan's large feet to the side. He was still wearing his boots.

I didn't sleep because Yvan coughed uncontrollably throughout the night. Sometimes I lost consciousness, but then the image of being surrounded by monstrous, ravenous people played out in my mind and I awoke terrified. I didn't know who they were or what they wanted. I sat up and glanced at the oppressive environment outside the window. The trees were as sad and poor as the people. A couple were standing outside on the street and shouting obscenities at one another. I looked beside me to see Yvan sleeping peacefully. His face was quiet and innocent like a baby's, but he'd get caught up in coughing fits every now and again. When it was day and Yvan was awake, I felt Yvan's forehead with my hand. He was burning hot and sure to die today or tomorrow. I walked into the bathroom and turned on the bathroom sink. Soon Yvan was shouting from the bedroom about all the things he needed to do today, but then he became so exhausted that he fell asleep again. Later that day, Yvan's father called me on the telephone. I didn't know how he got the number to Bambi's house. Yvan must have called his father while he was in town and given him the number to Bambi's landline. "Are you poisoning Yvan?" Mr. Prevost asked. I didn't say anything at first, but then I laughed because there wasn't anything to say.

As Yvan slept, I grabbed the teddy bear and carried him downstairs to the kitchen. Bambi had already shown me how to make the gingerbread people with the gingerbread mix that she'd prepared. All that was left for me to do was to shape the gingerbread men and women into appropriate figures on the baking tray, attire them with icing, and place the tray into the oven. After I did all that and placed the tray into the oven's mouth, I took the teddy bear from the stool by the kitchen island where he'd been sitting and I brought him with me into the living room. I turned on the television and waited for it to buzz on. The rainstorm had passed, and outside the living room window the rose bushes were knitted into the wild and nauseating landscape. On the TV news, a journalist was droning on about an abandoned alfalfa farm that was being turned into a carnival site, and the person the journalist was speaking to was explaining that the first thing to do when planning on turning a farm into a recreational site was to hire a consultant to advise you on how to obtain all the necessary things cheaply. This man was the owner of the carnival site. "Consultants cost money, but you save money in the long term when you hire them," the owner said. I watched the news program until the end. Then I ran to the kitchen in a panic because I thought I'd burnt the gingerbread people, but then I remembered Bambi's warning that this particular gingerbread mix had a lot of spice so you'll think you're burning the cookies but it's really just that there's too much ginger. I looked inside the oven's mouth and the gingerbread people were fine. I straightened Teddy's black bowtie, and we returned to the living room.

We watched the morning talk shows. When the gingerbread people were done, I returned to the kitchen. Opening the oven door, I removed the handsomest of all the gingerbread people from the baking tray. He really was set apart from the others. He was still warm and I burnt my fingers, but I didn't mind. I brought the gingerbread man to my mouth: eating first the legs, then the crotch, and finally the head with its symmetrical eyes of white icing. The eyes seemed to sadden as the gingerbread man's head neared my mouth. The cookie mixture was moist and it was devastating to think that tomorrow I might not remember what it tasted like.

The morning talk show ended with a cheerful

jingle and an audience laugh track, and then the TV displayed an image of Teddy and me standing in Bambi's house. I'm holding Teddy under my arm and his don't-forget-to-take-me-with-you eyes are turned up wistfully toward the wood beam ceiling. The television screen displays my life as it is at present. It's me standing in a room with Teddy. Then the static buzzes and I can see Teddy and me standing amidst the carnival that the man created from the former alfalfa farm. Beyond the rides, you can see the farms that haven't been abandoned yet. There's a line of slim trees separating the carnival site from these farms, and in the parking lot people are smoking electric cigarettes because they're bored with the carnival rides. They don't like Virginia Slims. They've never heard of them. The tilt-a-whirl is spinning at a breakneck speed and there's already a long line for the helter skelter. A girl with beautiful dark hair is standing in line and holding the hand of a child, but then the child gets angry about something it sees and yanks its hand away. People can be cruel. There's a life-size gingerbread house at the carnival, made entirely out of gingerbread, and inside are smaller gingerbread houses for sale starting at $200 apiece. I walk with Teddy into the gingerbread house, and the other people inside seem gleeful at first, picking gum drops and brownies from the gingerbread walls. They're deciding which of the smaller gingerbread houses they want to buy. Then something flashes in their eyes and they became enraged. They're soon ferocious, clawing at one another's clothes and skin. I glance around for Yvan, but he isn't there. I run outside the gingerbread house and shout for Yvan, but he's walking away. He turns around to me calling his name and he's just as superhuman as he was when I'd first seen him. "Au revoir, Charlotte," he says. "Au revoir." He's smiling and waving at me, and then he turns forward again and his boxing shoes plod against the wild, virgin land.